GOING
POSTAL

ANGSTROM PRESS

COVER DESIGN

Angstrom Press

EDITOR

Barbara Goffman

ISBN-13: 978-0692646236
ISBN-10: 069264623X

"You've got mail—there's something about that phrase that gets your adrenaline pumping. When a letter or package arrives, questions immediately arise: Is it a gift from your love? Or for him? A plea for help? An invitation to change your life? Or is it something you can't even imagine?

The six stories in this anthology take up these questions with gusto. They are in turn heartfelt and fantastical, solemn and funny. They may leave you ready to write your own letter or run out to check your mailbox, hoping that something fabulous is waiting for you. But you don't need to go to the post office to experience the joy of receiving a special delivery—this book provides six of them, and they're waiting for you."

~Barb Goffman, Editor

GOING POSTAL

A ROCKVILLE WRITERS' GROUP ANTHOLOGY

CONTENTS

AN UNEXPECTED GIFT

J. D. Cannon

Summer 1944
Glen Cove, New York

It was after two in the morning when Anna Kuznetsova stepped into the bedroom, her slim body wrapped in a thick white bath towel. Clouds of steam briefly followed her before dissolving in the cooler bedroom air. The party had gone on until well past midnight. She had been on her feet the whole time and was looking forward to some much-needed sleep.

She ran a hand through her short blond hair, still damp, and surveyed the furnishings of her room, as she had every night for the past few weeks, still barely able to believe her good fortune. Light gray wallpaper with white-stemmed roses the color of raspberries gave the room a decidedly feminine look. An antique dressing table of dark mahogany mated perfectly with a pair of matching end tables that flanked the single bed. Two small antique lamps atop the end tables painted the room with a soft light colored warm by the fringed ivory shades.

The room had a simple, understated elegance, and Anna had become very fond of it. She'd never dreamed she would be living in such a place. The room was small, but it was hers alone…at least for the remainder of summer. It was the first time in her twenty years that she hadn't had to share with anyone. The other servants slept three to a room, above the garage, and shared a single bathroom. Anna felt privileged to have these private quarters in the main house.

"Well, good evening," a man said, startling her. "Or should I say good morning."

Theodore "Teddy" van Nostrand III leaned against the closed bedroom door, looking his usual confident—and slightly inebriated—self. His bow tie was undone and his white tuxedo jacket was slung over his right shoulder, hanging casually from a long index finger.

"What…what are you doing here?"

"Well, my dear, I should think it's obvious. I've come to see you."

"This is my room." She wrapped her arms tightly around the towel. "You shouldn't be here."

"And this is my house." He paused and tilted his head as if he'd just had a clever thought. "Well, at least it's Father's house. Close enough, I suppose." He chuckled.

"You must leave now. At once. Or…or…"

Anna wanted to say that she would scream, but was afraid that if she did she might get into trouble or even lose her job.

"Shh." He put a finger to his lips and took a step closer.

Staring at the floor, she gripped the towel and stepped back.

"You know, Anna, I find you quite beautiful." He grabbed her left hand and stared at the brown mole on it. "Almost perfect, in fact."

She yanked her hand back.

He advanced another step. Then another. Anna's retreat was blocked by the dressing table.

He closed the distance and put a finger under her chin. He lifted her head, forcing her eyes to meet his.

"I just want to kiss you. That's all." He smiled.

She shook her head emphatically and broke his stare.

"That's all," he repeated.

She shook her head again.

"Well, then. Let me ask you something. Do you like this room?"

She remained silent.

"Do you?" he demanded.

She nodded.

"You know, it's much better living here than over the garage. Having to breathe those awful gasoline fumes and whatnot."

Anna's knees began to shake.

"Why, I'll bet that new Irish tart, what's her name, Bridget? Well, I'll bet she'd like this room just fine. And I'm quite certain she'd know how to show her appreciation."

"I didn't ask for this room," Anna said, eyes fixed on her bare feet standing on the expensive burgundy carpet. "Madame wanted me to have it."

"At my suggestion, no less."

She did not respond.

"Look now, just once. That's all I want. Then, I'll go."

He blew a kiss into the air. "See, just like that. Whatya' say?"

Anna stood silently, weighing her options. Finally, she conceded with a barely perceptible nod.

Teddy's mouth curled into a victor's smile. He let his jacket fall to the floor as he cradled her face in his hands. She closed her eyes as he kissed her, trying not to acknowledge it was happening.

He kissed her lips gently.

"See that wasn't so bad, was it?" he said, smiling.

She couldn't look at him.

"I think you'll like this one even more." The tone of his voice turned menacing.

He grabbed her shoulders and pulled her toward him. She stiffened and tried to resist, but she was no match for his strength. He kissed her roughly and tried to part her lips with his tongue.

"No. Please...please, no."

His smile vanished, replaced by a sneer. He ripped the towel from her body, grabbed her shoulders roughly, and threw her onto the bed.

"If you like your job, you'll be quiet," he warned. "Who knows, you might even enjoy it."

He let the towel drop to the floor and approached.

Anna whimpered and curled into a fetal position, a futile attempt to protect her virtue and her nakedness. But he was too fast, and too strong. His nicotine-yellowed fingers covered her mouth as he forced her legs apart with his knees.

Anna tried her best to blot out the pain and humiliation of what followed. But the stench of stale whiskey and tobacco would stay with her forever.

#

J. D. Cannon

Scranton, Pennsylvania
Six months later

The building was plain and looked to be a perfect square. It sat atop a small swell of earth void of any shrubs or decoration and was surrounded by a ring of dead brown grass. The building was made of a cold, stark, unwelcoming gray stone that matched the color and mood of the December day.

With an icy wind to her back, and her blond hair blowing straight out in front of her, Anna carried the small suitcase and hurried after her mother. At the end of the concrete walkway, they climbed three low steps to the main entrance of the building. Anna's mother paused to catch her breath and then pulled at the heavy door of half glass and half wood. At first the door wouldn't give. Her mother tugged at it again with all her weight, and the door finally gave way with a whoosh. They entered.

"Wait here," Anna's mother said to her in Russian. She did not look at Anna. Then she disappeared behind a door to the right with the words Office & Reception stenciled in black paint.

Anna set her suitcase down. Its rusted metal hinges made a clacking sound against the black marble floor. She took in the lobby...at least that's what she assumed it would be called. She guessed that it was about fifteen feet wide and thirty feet deep, with a high ceiling...at least fifteen feet high, she thought. The height made the space feel quite large. An old chandelier, the color of unpolished brass, hung from the ceiling, its six gray-white bulbs unlit at this time of day. The walls were of plaster and were painted a drab shade of institutional green. Not counting the main entrance door, there was one door to the right of where she stood, the one her mother had used, and one directly in front of her. The word Private had been stenciled on it. Both doors, as well as the interior side of the entrance door were painted to match the color of the walls. One plain wooden straight-backed chair was placed at the center of the left wall with a simple wooden crucifix mounted on the wall directly above it.

The cold draft spilling in from the entrance contributed to the mood of the room. The draft's one saving grace was that it made the reek of disinfectant more tolerable.

Anna went to the entrance door and looked out at the black sedan that had brought her and her mother to this place. She could see it idling in the semicircular driveway at the end of the walk. Puffs of white exhaust drifted upward and were quickly caught and dissolved by the wind. The driver's window was cracked open, and the fetid smoke from his cigarette blended with the exhaust as it billowed out into the frigid air.

Anna paced the room and then sat for a spell. She repeated this several times—whenever the sitting became boring or uncomfortable. She had no idea how long she waited, but it was quite some time. When her mother finally reappeared, she stood as the older woman approached.

They stared at each other, neither saying a word. Anna searched her mother's eyes for a glimmer of warmth, love, or anything at all. But there was nothing.

"Here you will stay until you have the child," her mother finally said. "Then you may come home." She paused before continuing. "Alone!"

"But…"

"Shh. That is enough. It has been arranged."

Anna's mother stepped closer, placed her hands on Anna's shoulders, and kissed her hard, once on each cheek. Then she turned and left.

Anna watched her mother walk to the waiting car and did her best to hold back the tears. Seconds later, the Office & Reception door opened and a nun in black habit entered the lobby, closing the door behind her. She was about Anna's height, overweight, and wore no smile or kindness on her face. Her hands disappeared inside the long sleeves of her habit as she stared at Anna over small wire-rimmed glasses.

"Come with me," she demanded, more than invited.

Anna just looked at her, not knowing what to think, as the nun turned on a heel and clacked across the lobby toward the door marked Private.

Anna was still staring, numbed and frightened, when the nun reached the door.

"Come with me," she barked. "Right now!"

Anna could no longer hold back her tears.

#

Brooklyn, New York
December 1969

As she did every day, Anna stood at her apartment's sole window, leaning into it slightly. Her hands, covered with coarse black woolen gloves, gripped each side of the window frame and helped to support her weight. A brown babushka covered her graying hair.

She looked to the south and recognized the T-shaped structure that would serve as her reference point. Today the parachute jump ride at Coney Island was barely visible in the morning haze. Anna looked to the east of the landmark. She really couldn't see anything recognizable, but she knew it was there, less than two miles to the east: Brighton Beach, Brooklyn, also known as Little Odessa. It was where she had grown up after coming to America. Her sister Svetlana and a few cousins still lived there, though not in the tenements they had shared as children.

Anna closed her eyes and allowed the sun to warm her face as her thoughts traveled back to an earlier time and place and the things that might have been. For a few minutes…she never knew how long the trip would last…she was oblivious to the hiss and honk of the cars and trucks speeding by on the Brooklyn-Queens Expressway, which was a stone's throw from her window. Anna was never the same after her stay at the orphanage. Somehow word had gotten out about what had happened to her, and Anna was considered damaged goods by potential suitors, leaving her to grow into womanhood alone. Having no education, the best she could do was to resume her occupation as a servant. She was fortunate to find a wealthy family that kept her employed for two decades, and who provided her with a small pension when she was replaced with a younger, prettier woman. The pension was barely enough to subsist on, but Anna was grateful for their generosity nevertheless.

A thick cloud drifting in from the west blotted out the sunlight and brought Anna back to the present. Her return to reality was reinforced by the unmistakable smell of cabbage soup that had begun to simmer on the hot plate that sat atop her small Formica table. She left the window and slowly made her way over to check on the breakfast.

Svetlana and Yuri had invited her to breakfast today, but she had declined. Anna glanced at the orange hands of the clock radio. They would come for her in thirty minutes. Three times this morning she was tempted to walk to the pay phone in the hallway and call them to cancel. Now it was too late. Besides, it wouldn't have been fair to Yuri after he had been so helpful.

She turned toward the single bed at the opposite side of the room and thought about putting on the black dress she had laid out now, before she had her breakfast, but she changed her mind. She didn't want the dress to smell like the soup. Not only would that be embarrassing, but she would then have to have the dress cleaned. And she couldn't afford that. She wasn't worried about the housedress she was wearing, though. It was once a lively pink color dotted with blue and yellow flowers, but it had long since faded into a hodgepodge of dingy patterns that were hard to recognize. She would just soak it in the sink to get rid of the cabbage smell.

Anna took a spoon and a small chipped bowl from the shelf above the table, poured some soup, and sat down to eat. She turned on the radio and tried to separate the news and weather report from the AM static. She finished the soup, washed the spoon and bowl in the sink, and changed.

From across the room, Anna stared at the large envelope neatly placed at the corner of the table. She remembered the day it had arrived, addressed to *Occupant*. Anna knew junk mail when she saw it and rarely opened those unwanted parcels. But this package was different. She was drawn to the picture of the dark boy on the front of the envelope, his large eyes staring back with sadness. Through the sadness, Anna thought she saw a flicker of hope, and it compelled her to open the package and read its contents…a cover letter and a collection of photographs and forms. The cover letter contained a larger picture of the boy, this time holding what looked to be an empty tin cup. Anna now knew the letter by heart, particularly the words below his picture.

What Will Diego Eat Today?
Probably nothing. He has no family. He must
beg for food. Every year, hundreds of orphaned

children die from hunger or exposure to the elements.

Please, don't let Diego be one of them.

The letter went on to ask that Diego be sponsored by pledging a recurring annual sum, payable in affordable monthly installments. If he got a sponsor, Diego's basic food and necessities could be provided and he would survive. Anna had read that letter at least a hundred times. And each time it made her cry. She cried for Diego. She cried because she was not in a position to help him. And she cried because it brought her thoughts back to that awful day when the gray-faced nuns took her son from her arms as she napped, not even offering a chance to say good-bye.

Anna sat on the edge of the bed and looked at her left hand. The mole was large and brown, almost the size of a half dollar. She thought about what she would initiate today…and whether she really wanted to do it after so much time had passed. Svetlana had been trying to convince her for almost a year now, ever since Anna had shared her secret. Finally, two weeks ago, Anna had conceded. She would try to find her son.

A tear dripped its way down her cheek and rested at the corner of her mouth. She wiped the salty droplet with the back of her hand and looked at the mole once again. Anna had always been self-conscious about it. When she was a little girl and complained about it, her mother told her it was a gift from God. He thought she was much more special than other people, so he marked her so she would stand out and he could easily recognize her when he looked down from heaven. Fortunately, as she grew into womanhood, the mole was overshadowed by Anna's natural beauty and personality, and no one seemed to even notice it. Now, however, she thought it was an eyesore, just like the rest of her. She often wondered how her son would cope with it in his life. He was born with an identical marking.

Anna's thoughts were interrupted by three rapid knocks on her door.

"Anna. Anna it's me," Svetlana called. "Are you ready?"

She unchained and opened the door and let her sister in.

"Hello, my dear," Svetlana said as they embraced and exchanged kisses on both cheeks. "Yuri is waiting outside. We have just heard on the news there is a bad accident on the BQE, so we will have to take another way. We must hurry or we will be late. Come, let's get your coat."

Svetlana was dressed in a dark colored fur coat and matching hat and looked very fashionable. Her husband, Yuri, was a successful furrier. Svetlana's black high-heeled shoes were new and were no doubt the latest style, but Anna wouldn't know anything about that.

Anna went to the bed and picked up her black coat.

"Anna, Anna. It is below freezing outside. You'll catch your death of cold in that coat. Why don't you let me give you one that is warmer? You should have something that will keep you warm, especially now. Maybe fur. I will ask Yuri."

"And where would I wear it?" Anna said, shaking her head as she put on the coat. They had had this conversation before.

Twenty minutes later, Yuri's gleaming 1968 black Cadillac backed into the empty space in front of the Brooklyn Heights brownstone. He straightened the wheels and pulled forward a few feet, then backed up so that the car was perfectly centered between an old Mercedes and a banged-up Buick.

"See, Anna, what luck," Yuri said. "Can you believe that…a parking space right in front of his office? I think this is a good omen, yes?"

Anna was too nervous. She said nothing.

They climbed the six marble steps to the entrance, and Yuri pressed the doorbell that was just to the right of the brass plaque engraved with *Shaw, Epstein, and Raab*. A few seconds later they were buzzed in and entered an elegant foyer with a highly polished hardwood floor and an expensive-looking Oriental rug. An attractive, well-dressed young woman appeared almost immediately from a room off to the side.

"Good morning, Mr. Brumel. How are you today?"

"Good morning, Stephanie. I am good, thank you. And yourself?"

"Just fine. It's good to see you again. Mr. Barton is ready for you. May I get anyone coffee or tea?"

Yuri looked at Anna and Svetlana. They shook their heads.

"No, I think we are fine, thank you."

"Well then, please follow me."

Todd Barton looked to be in his late twenties. He was about six feet tall with straight blond hair parted to the side, and had sky-blue eyes. He was dressed in a dark blazer, light-blue shirt, and charcoal slacks. His maroon and white rep necktie had a perfect Windsor knot. He rose, warmly greeted Yuri, and politely shook hands with the women as Yuri introduced them. He invited everyone to sit in the three antique captain's chairs that were set in front of his desk. Barton and Yuri exchanged a bit of small talk, and Yuri indicated his pleasure with the outcome of the lease negotiations that Barton had handled for Yuri's newest store.

"So, how may I help you today, Yuri?"

"Actually, the help we need is for my sister-in-law, Anna," Yuri said, nodding in Anna's direction.

"I see." Barton turned to Anna and smiled. "And how may I be of help, Anna?"

Anna briefly met his eyes and then looked down. An uncomfortable silence followed.

"Anna," Yuri asked, "would you like me to speak for you?"

She nodded.

"Very well," Yuri said. "Then I think it is best to start at the beginning."

Yuri briefed the lawyer on the facts and events that had transpired decades earlier. Barton listened intently, occasionally jotting notes on a yellow legal pad. Finally, Yuri got to the reason they were here today.

"Anna would like to make contact with her son," he said.

Barton stopped taking notes. He looked at both Yuri and Anna before speaking.

"I see."

"Can you help Anna, Mr. Barton?" Yuri asked.

Barton took a deep breath, and looked at Anna, who returned his look with hopeful eyes.

"I can certainly try, but I must be very candid with you. I have some experience in these matters. I think the chances are very slim, at best, that the orphanage will release the kind of information that you seek. Particularly since it's a Catholic orphanage. They tend to be very uncooperative in my experience."

Anna's eyes dropped to her lap as Barton said this.

"Anna, did you sign any papers at the orphanage? Papers that would give up your rights as the boy's mother? That sort of thing?" Barton asked.

"There were many papers to sign." Anna nodded. "Many papers." She shook her head. "I have no memory of what they said." After an awkward silence, she looked at him.

"I'm very sorry," Barton said slowly. He looked at Yuri, then at Anna. "I really don't think there's much I can do."

A tear fell down Anna's cheek.

"Couldn't we take them to court?" Yuri asked, his voice full of hope.

"On what basis?" Barton replied.

"Well, I don't know. I was hoping you could think of something," Yuri said.

"Yuri, even if we could find a reason, it would be a long and drawn out process. Expensive as well."

"I am not concerned about the money," Yuri said. "How long?"

"Probably six months to a year. Something like that."

"No," Yuri said, closing his eyes and shaking his head. "We don't have that much time."

Barton raised his eyebrows, a confused look on his face.

"We don't have that kind of time," Yuri repeated. "Anna. She is sick. She doesn't have much time left."

"Oh." Barton shifted his gaze between Yuri and Anna. "I'm so sorry to hear that."

"Mr. Barton, isn't there anything you can do to help Anna? Anything at all?" Svetlana pleaded.

Barton let out a heavy sigh and pursed his lips. He stood and walked around to the front of his desk and approached Anna, whose tears were flowing freely. He took her hand in both of his.

"Anna," he said, "Anna…"

Barton's words were deafened by the pounding of Anna's heart. She stared, trance-like, at the mole on his left hand. It was identical to hers. God's gift to them both.

EVERYTHING MUST GO

Stella Donovan

They'd met in Cairo four years earlier trying to steal the same painting. They'd each planned a solo heist, but after a violent tussle that involved frame cutters, wire clippers, and a grappling hook, they decided to combine their talents.

They'd been together ever since.

The painting, valued at sixty million dollars, hung on the wall of their shared apartment. They estimated it would be another three years before they could safely sell it on the black market. Until then, they'd resolved to work their office jobs, socialize with their friends, and attempt to cultivate legal hobbies.

Things became quiet and miserable.

He was unable to stop eating. She was unable to stop shopping.

The worst part, he thought, was that the whole canvas was an eyesore. Small wonder the painter had cut his ear off.

#

She planned to break up with him in early June, three tasteful weeks before their lease ended. In her opinion, it was the ideal amount of time to divide their belongings, find separate living arrangements, and cry through a final round of break-up sex. She had every intention of going through with it. She browsed for apartments on her work computer. She drafted a brief bio for a dating website. And then, sometime in late May, she lost her nerve.

#

He planned to break up with her in early June, three tasteful weeks before their lease ended. It was the only date he could find that didn't conflict with any major holidays, birthdays, or family functions. He had every intention of going through with it. He made quiet arrangements to move in with a friend. He maneuvered next to his attractive coworker during happy hour. And then, sometime in late May, he lost his nerve.

#

A week before they moved to their new apartment, she sat with him on the couch while he watched football. She waited for a commercial.

"There's a Degas exhibit in Poland this weekend," she began. "Some of them are worth thirty-two million."

As she'd predicted, he kept his eyes on the television. In the past few months, she'd noticed that he'd stopped looking at her when she spoke to him.

"You know we have to stay small and local," he told her.

"Well, there's also a Cézanne exhibit in—"

"I thought we decided to focus on the Matisse lithograph."

"No, you decided to focus on the Matisse lithograph," she answered. "It's not even signed. My Christmas bonus will bring in more money than an unsigned litho—"

"Can we talk about this later? I just want to watch the game."

"Fine," she said, taking out her phone and opening the website for the local home store.

E-commerce was her only refuge. She couldn't trust herself to shop in stores. Mall security was too easy to bypass. She knew she'd be tempted to indulge in the rush of a steal. It would only take one lapse to trigger the downward spiral. She wouldn't be able to stop. She knew that she'd eventually get caught stealing a three dollar sandwich with five dollars in her pocket. It was an undignified eventuality for a thief who couldn't quit. So she shopped online, channeling her energy into finding bargains, even if they were for things she didn't necessarily need. Getting something cheaply felt like a form of stealing. Sometimes it felt like the only form of excitement she had left.

"You're shopping again," he said, startling her.

"How do you know that?"

"You have that predatory focus thing. Like a cheetah stalking a gazelle."

"I don't see why it's any of your business what I do with my money," she said, returning her gaze to the phone.

"It's very important that we don't look like we're living outside our means right now."

"I know that. I'm looking for a set of closet organizers. I'm not buying a Bentley."

"Oh, you're buying stuff to organize your stuff," he said. "Makes sense."

"Our stuff. We won't have as much storage space in the new apartment. Why are we even talking about this? I thought you wanted to watch the game."

She continued swiping through the carousel of neatly ordered items.

She found the OmniBox on the last page of search results. It was advertised as an all-in-one home organization system, but it didn't have a picture or any additional product descriptions. Though it had received a five-star rating from over two million users, no one had left a review. This made her suspicious. She couldn't remember the last time she'd seen something on the Internet that wasn't accompanied by an endless stream of opinions. She was about to circle back to her earlier favorites when she saw its price.

"For your information," she told him, "I just found a total home organization system for a dollar."

Satisfied, she ordered the OmniBox with a single click.

#

He was home alone when the package arrived the next day. He was looking in the mirror, pinching his midsection and examining his torso from different angles. He'd observed a disciplined diet-and-exercise regime when he was actively thieving, keeping himself in prime shape for the heists that he planned. After they'd stolen the painting and retired, it was liberating to eat what he wanted and skip workouts without worrying about immediate consequences. But unhealthy foods became harder to resist the more he indulged in them, and the weight came on at a rate it never had before. Standing in front of the mirror, he no longer recognized himself.

Three sharp knocks on the front door interrupted his reverie. He opened the door and saw a large black box with bright red corners at his feet. It came up to his to his navel and looked similar to the cardboard boxes he was packing for their move to the new apartment. The box was both unlabeled and unsealed, its two top panels lifting slightly upward. He looked down the hallway for the mailman. The corridor was empty.

Assuming it was something she'd ordered, he stooped down and wrapped his arms around the edges of the box. He braced himself for an awkward, heavy lift and straightened his legs. To his surprise, the box was almost weightless.

He carried the box to the coffee table in the living room. He glanced inside its panels. It was empty. He knew he should leave it alone so she could rectify her botched delivery, but something about the box unnerved him. There was something eerie about its inky-black sides, its blood-red corners. He decided to take it to the building's garbage room before she got home. He emptied the apartment's trash cans and gathered all the waste into one large trash bag. He dropped the bag into the box and turned to grab his keys from a hook on the wall. When he looked back, the box was empty.

#

When she got home from work, she found him pacing in front of a large black box with red corners.

"What's that?" she asked.

"What did you order?"

Here it was, she thought. The inquisition that followed each of her purchases.

"Just the home organizer," she answered. "That was only a dollar. And definitely doesn't look outside our means."

"Is this it?" he asked, indicating the black box.

"I'm not sure. There wasn't a picture. I think it was called an OmniBox?"

"And you're sure the ad said it was an organizer?"

"Uh, yes. In addition to finding bargains, I can also read."

"Okay, look, this is going to sound crazy."

"What is?"

"The box was empty when it got delivered, so I was going to throw it out. I put a bag of trash inside of it to get rid of all our garbage at once, and the bag just disappeared."

"What do you mean 'disappeared?'" she asked.

"The box, like, ate it. I thought I was going crazy, so I tossed a set of your bookends inside, and—"

"The mermaid ones I just bought?"

"Yeah, and they disappeared, too."

She narrowed her eyes. She knew he hadn't liked the bookends. He hadn't even been impressed when she'd told him they were fifty percent off.

"If you were going to get rid of my bookends, you could at least have thought of something more plausible than a magical box."

"I'm serious," he insisted. "They just vanished."

"Right, like we've never made anything vanish before."

She picked up a book off the coffee table and tossed it inside the box. She didn't hear it land. She looked down and saw that the box was empty.

"Okay," she conceded. "That was weird. Give me your phone."

"Why?"

"Just do it."

He surrendered his phone.

"Is it on full volume?" she asked.

"Yeah,"

"Good," she said, dropping it into the box.

He flinched. "Why did you do that?"

"I know how these boxes work. It's a trick. It has a secret compartment. A false bottom or something. It's probably a gag gift. That's why it was only a dollar. Sometimes you get what you pay for."

She took out her phone and called his number.

"It's ringing," she told him.

She stared at the box, waiting to hear his phone ring. There was silence. Her call went to his voice mail.

She tried his phone number again. This time, the call didn't connect at all.

#

He felt around the inside of the box with his hands, searching for his phone.

"How deep does this thing go?" he muttered. "It's so cold in here."

He stuck his head into the blackness of the box's interior. A fragrance enveloped him, overwhelming his senses. Lavender. He leaned farther in and inhaled. The smell traveled up through his nose and down the length of his body. He felt a surge of joy. He inhaled again. He let out a loud, buoyant laugh.

His laugh echoed back to him.

Startled, he jumped away from the box and fell back onto their sofa.

"What on earth was that?" she asked.

"There's no bottom," he answered after a moment. "It's a void. "A black hole. An abyss."

"What? Are you sure?"

"I'm positive. You saw it yourself."

"Okay, I don't know what this thing is, but I want it out of here. Now."

He knew he should agree, but the smell of lavender lingered around him.

"Well, hang on," he said. "Let's not be hasty."

"I think haste is completely called for in this situation."

He looked around the apartment, taking in the piles of unwanted items they needed to pack or discard before the move.

"We have a lot of stuff we need to get rid of before we leave," he told her.

"Yeah. In a dumpster. Or a charity."

"But if the box is here, we might as well use it," he said. "And then we'll get rid of it right after."

He knew he was lying as he said it. He also knew that, for some reason, he didn't care.

"I guess it would save us an errand," she said after a brief hesitation. "We still have a lot of packing to do."

"I could start in the kitchen," he volunteered.

"I could see if there's anything in the bedroom. But we get rid of it right after we're done. Deal?"

"Deal," he confirmed.

#

She went to her closet and started with her bridesmaid's dresses, the hulking yards of tulle and chiffon that she would never wear again. As she dropped them into the box, a scent wafted out of it. Vanilla. She knelt down next to the box and inhaled again. Her mood soared. She breathed in the fragrance again and again, unable to remember a time when she had smelled anything so wonderful. When she returned to her closet, she no longer recognized its contents. Each article used to have its own personality, its own relationship to the shape of her body. Now the space looked like an indistinguishable sea of wasted fabric. How had she ever thought that one body needed so many clothes? She stripped the hangers and gutted her drawers and shelves, throwing pile after pile of clothes into the box. She dropped them into the darkness and felt free.

#

He started with the cookies, those small lapses in his dietary discipline that triggered his larger binges. He took a last look at them, packaged in their neat, sugary rows, perfectly ridged and identical, and carried them to the box. As soon as they disappeared, a strange, euphoric lightness came over him. How, he wondered, had he ever craved cookies?

He purged the rest of the kitchen, clearing out the butter, the white bread, the red meat, the processed cheeses, and the microwaveable breakfast sandwiches. He dropped them into the darkness and felt free.

#

The next morning, she went to work in the clothes she'd worn the day before. She was tired. They'd spent most of the night prowling through each room of their apartment, getting rid of anything that would fit in the box. They fed the box their dining sets, their mugs, and all of their utensils. After that, they'd moved on to the larger and more expensive items. Their nightstands, their laptops, their bookshelves, and their televisions were all gone. She hadn't felt that invigorated since their last heist.

But at her office, she felt surrounded by clutter. Her drawers were crammed with more office supplies than she could ever use. By lunchtime she couldn't take it anymore.

She took a cardboard box from the office's warehouse and cleaned out her desk.

When she got home, she found that the box had expanded. It was at least two feet taller and three feet wider than it had been the day before. She gave it all the clutter from her workstation, but she didn't feel as empty and peaceful as she had the day before. She sensed that it needed more. She felt embarrassed, ashamed that she had nothing else to offer.

And then she remembered the painting.

#

"I rode through the desert for five days on an extremely uncomfortable camel to get that painting out of Egypt, and you just threw it away?"

He was talking to her on his office phone, his hand clenched around the receiver.

"Okay, maybe I should have talked to you first," she said.

"Maybe you shouldn't have thrown sixty million dollars down the fucking toilet," he hissed.

One of his coworkers looked over at him. He tried to keep his face neutral.

"I didn't throw it down the toilet. I gave it the box."

"That was our security," he whispered. "That was our retirement. That was a van-fucking-Gogh."

"It was the only thing that felt worthy. I don't know what's happening to me. It's that box. I can't think straight when I'm around it. It has this, this—"

Suddenly, he understood.

"Smell," he finished, leaning his forehead against his palm. "A smell that makes you crazy."

"Like vanilla."

"It's lavender for me," he said, sighing. "This whole thing is my fault. You knew something was off about that box. You wanted to get rid of it, and I stopped you."

"Well, at least now we don't have to worry about looking like we live outside our means. We don't have any means. Or furniture. Or any other clothes. I'm calling you from a freaking pay phone. We're at the end of our rope."

"Our rope," he echoed softly, sitting up straighter.

"What did you say?"

"Maybe it's not too late," he said.

"How?"

"Do you still have that rappelling system we used in Monaco?" he asked. "For the Rembrandt job?"

#

She strapped him into the harness and secured the system's anchor to one of the railings on their patio.

"What if it's like a space black hole?" he asked her. "Won't my body get shredded?"

"You stuck your face in there when we first got it," she answered, heaving the large pile of rope onto the ground near the anchor. "It's just like a regular hole."

"Well, what if the anchor fails? I'd fall forever, slowly starving to death."

"The anchor isn't going to fail," she reassured him. "You checked it yourself. Just go down as far as the rope will take you, and then come right back up."

She helped him rig the ropes through the descender.

"Wish me luck," he told her.

"You don't need it. Just breathe through your mouth."

As she watched, he took a deep breath and lowered himself into the box.

"Still whole?" she called down after his head disappeared.

"So far," came the muffled answer.

She stepped away from the box and kept her eyes on the anchoring system. She tried to ignore the fragrance that surrounded her, but she came to an unsettling realization as the minutes passed.

The farther he lowered himself down, the lighter she felt.

#

It was wet and dark inside the box. The small circle of light at the box's opening seemed miles away. After a few minutes, he was unable see the ropes in front of his face. As his anxiety built, he forgot to breathe through his mouth. He knew that the painting was gone and he should start the ascent. He knew he should return to his apartment and his girlfriend, but, after a few minutes, he found that he didn't want to. The smell was intoxicating. The darkness began to feel warm and comforting.

#

Strange thoughts clouded her mind. If the anchor failed and he dropped, she thought, nothing could implicate her. She could tape the box shut. Take it to a landfill. Start over with someone new. Be someone new. She wasn't getting any younger. She was running out of time and chances.

Lost in thought, she drifted onto the patio, moving slowly toward the anchor.

#

His thoughts grew more disjointed as he descended. He could no longer recall his name or anything about himself. He felt marvelously unburdened. He was falling asleep. He wanted to fall asleep. He knew he could have this warm feeling forever if he just unclipped himself from the rope. His hand reached for the side of the harness.

#

She began to loosen the anchor. Just as she was about to dislodge the system, she felt something wet hit her forehead. She wiped it with her hand and stared down at her fingers. The liquid was white and soupy. She looked up and saw a bird perched on the tree limb above her. She gagged and left the anchor attached to the patio railing.

She ran inside and held her face under the kitchen faucet. As she scrubbed her face, the smell of the vanilla faded. She realized the severity of what she had almost done, and, for the first time, registered how much time had passed since he'd descended.

She ran back to the box. She cupped her hands around her mouth and shouted as loud as she could.

"Come back! Come back!"

She shouted again and again, making herself hoarse. After a few minutes, she finally heard the sounds of his ascent.

#

He told her later that, at the very moment he was about to let go, her voice had awakened him. No matter how many times he asked, she refused to tell him how she'd recovered her senses.

They taped the box shut as soon as he recovered from the climb, deadening the effect of the fragrance that leaked out the top. After the box was sealed, there was only one thing he wanted to do. They left the apartment and drove to the nearest mall, filling cart after cart with clothes, books, cutlery, electronics, and furniture. It was the first time he'd actually enjoyed shopping.

The next day, they loaded their moving van with their new purchases. They stood one last time in their empty apartment.

He found the courage to bring it up first.

"So what do we do with the box?" he asked her. "Burn it?"

"I'm not touching that thing again. And I don't want you going anywhere near it either."

"Well, we can't just leave it here."

"I think that's exactly what we should do. The building manager is going to have this place cleaned before someone else moves in. The cleaning crew will toss it out for us."

"I guess that seems like the safest option," he said, happy to embrace the alternative.

He lingered in the doorway of the apartment.

"What?" she asked.

"I was thinking, is that Degas exhibit still going on in Poland? We're going to need some new art on the walls."

#

The next day, a married couple moved in. The man found the box undisturbed in the living room. He picked it up, surprised at its lightness. He took out a pocketknife, sliced through the tape, and felt a draft hit his face. Confused, he called his wife over to see. Together they stared into its depths.

THE WEEKEND

Judy Kelly

Dina Covington stood outside Good As American Pie, the restaurant that her husband, Rick, owned. She always told everyone that he owned the restaurant, even though she put in many hours of overtime at her office to help him buy it. She stood at the heavy double-glass doors with her hand on the familiar glass handle, smiled slightly, took a deep breath, and then entered. After she stepped inside, she took a second to straighten her hip-hugging black skirt, Rick's favorite, wishing she had had the fortitude to stick with her diet. She puffed up her dark hair, and proceeded to the "Stop Here For Seating" sign.

She made it a point to arrive early, well before the heavy lunch crowd of business suits and ties, regulars from the surrounding corporations and loyal customers who patronized his restaurant. She hated to interrupt Rick during the busy times. She knew how he liked to give as much personal attention to his devoted customers as he could.

Dina loved going to the restaurant. It gave her a chance to reminisce about those days, twelve years ago, when Rick was a pastry chef, and she was a server, and every day they would sneak off to the cramped storage room to take their twenty-minute break. They fell in love in this restaurant, but when Rick changed it to the modern, upscale bistro it was now, Dina felt it wasn't the same romantic eatery that held them together. To her, when Rick added the high ceilings with skylights and fans, and maple wood furnishings the ambience changed.

During those days they had slipped away, they hadn't had much. She was a poor college student and he was a student at the renowned pastry college downtown. They had each other. He was her whole life, and she was his. Now he owned the four-star restaurant and she wasn't sure where they stood; things had changed; they had changed.

She turned left and started into the main dining room, but when she saw the time, she changed her mind and headed for the kitchen. On her way through the bar and just before the kitchen, she saw Rick walk toward the booth closest to the bar. She knew Rick liked to use that as his prep place when the bar was closed. She let out a smile when she saw he had on his favorite white apron, the one with a drawing of a chef's hat. It was the one she'd given him when they bought the restaurant seven years ago. Rick was doing something with the menus. Dina couldn't see exactly what, but she figured he was making changes for the evening.

"Hi, Rick." She eased out her words.

He turned and saw her. "Dina?"

She smiled and relaxed a little, thinking he was no longer angry with her even though the night before he went to bed angry at her. She had accused him, as she had done many times lately, of flirting—this time with the checker in the supermarket. Dina had told Rick that he wanted to get in her line so he could wink and flirt at her. Dina had seen the checker's hand touch his when he helped her bag the food.

"I bought you that pan that you said you wanted." She handed him a red and gold gift bag, but she was still a little nervous.

He took the bag, opened it, and peeped inside. "Dina, this is just the one I wanted." He reached over to kiss her. "Thanks honey."

"Now, before you say anything, I'm not staying, and I don't want to fight. I just came to say two things." She held up two fingers. "First, Rick, I'm sorry."

"I know, Dina," he began, "I know."

"I don't know why I…What's wrong with me?"

"Dina, don't—"

"What you said. You're right." She took his hand in hers.

"Dina, last night, I didn't mean—" He tightened his grip.

"It's been hard on you, too. I want to change."

"I know you do, but you're always on the defense. We can't keep going through the same thing. I mean I can't keep doing this. Understand?"

"I know. I don't wanna be that way. It just happens," she said, voice rising.

"Okay, sweetheart, okay. When you accuse me of being with other women, it hurts." He let go of her hand.

"I don't mean to do that. It's just you're so successful and nice and gorgeous." She tugged at her skirt again, pulled it down while trying to suck in her stomach.

"We both are. 'Together we are,' remember? You just got a promotion, and Dina, I think you're very beautiful. Sweetheart—"

"Rick, did you order an extra load of beef?" A server walking out from the kitchen yelled out. "Oh. Sorry."

Dina recognized Ellen dressed in her waitress uniform, the black skirt so short and tight, Dina wondered how she could move. Dina gave her a smile.

"There's a man out back who needs your signature for the extra beef you ordered. Am I waitressing the party?"

He stepped closer and kissed Dina on her forehead. "Sweetheart, I can't do this now. We can talk later."

"Okay," Dina said. She started toward the door, and then turned around. "Oh, I almost forgot, the second thing…" She halted when she saw Ellen standing close to Rick as he picked up a black leather-bound menu and held it out to her. He turned to Dina. Ellen whispered something funny when she took the book. She grabbed hold of Rick's arm and let out a loud laugh. He smiled back at her.

"Ellen, you remember my wife, Dina," Rick said.

Ellen smiled at Dina, gave Rick a bump with her hip, and leaned in to whisper in his ear again. He pulled back slightly, a scowl on his face. She moved closer to him, and for a moment, Dina thought Ellen was going to kiss her husband. They seemed so familiar with each other it was hard to believe that Ellen was just a waitress in his restaurant. This didn't look very good to Dina, and she promised herself that she would remain calm and not act the way she saw her mother mistreat her father, or the way she had the night before.

"I knew it," Dina yelled out. "I just knew it." So much for being calm and reasonable. Dina didn't care.

Rick gave his wife a pleading look.

"I knew something was happening. I just knew it."

"Dina, what are you talking about?"

"You two seem so cozy together. How long have you been seeing each other? Huh? How long?"

"Dina, we're—"

"You stupid pig. And you," she shouted out and pointed her finger to Ellen, "What are you, an idiot? Are you that desperate that you have to move in on someone's husband? You're too idiotic and such a lowlife that no one wants you?" Tears ran down Dina's face. "Rick, I came by to tell you that we should go to couple's therapy. But now I wonder if I'm really the one with the problem."

"Dina, Honey. You're doing it again."

"No, I see what I see. This woman is climbing all over you. It's clear that something is wrong. You can't stay away from women. That's what's wrong with our marriage."

"What...I...We were talking about—"

"About intimate things, it seems like." She turned to leave. "Don't bother coming home, Rick. We're through. This is the end. We just can't fix our marriage." She wiped at the tears on her face.

On her way out, she slowed down to take in the restaurant and the improvements he had made after he bought it seven years ago. The hanging chandeliers at every table, the smell of freshly polished solid oak floors, the glass-top bar—his pride and joy—modern art on the walls, all brought on more tears. If only he'd done that to his marriage, maybe this day would not have happened.

#

Dina arrived home to a small package underneath her mailbox. She picked it up. The fancy looking swirls and curls on the handwritten label made it difficult for her to read, and the package didn't have a return address. She hadn't ordered anything, and thinking the package was delivered to her in error, she looked around for a mailman. She saw him scurry across the street to the Martin home and ran to catch him before he went to the next house.

"Good afternoon," she said as the mail carrier came down to the sidewalk.

"Good afternoon," he said in return.

"You left this package at my door." She pointed to her house.

He looked at the package. "Does it have your name on it?"

"I didn't order anything. I can't read the address label and there's no return address or anything so I don't know how to send it back. It's not for me. I just want you to take it back."

"Ma'am, I can't do that. I didn't deliver this to you."

"But it was sitting at my house."

"There's no postal stamp, and I can't read the address either."

"But there's no sender." She pointed to the package.

"Keep it. There could be something valuable inside." He turned to continue his route.

#

Once inside, she put the package down on the mahogany coffee table in the airy living room and threw herself down on the floral couch. Was she ready to give up on her marriage? When they talked about it two weeks ago, and again the night before, Rick had suggested that they seek counseling. He said he wanted to try to make things work. She was so afraid she was turning into her mother, who bullied and abused her father every chance she got. Before they married, she told Rick all about her mother and her fear of becoming her. She never tried to hide it, and he told her that he loved her more for trusting him. Dina's fear was that she was driving Rick away from her the same way her mother had driven her father away. She was ashamed of herself. She had just called her husband a pig. That was the name her mother called her father when her mother found out that her father was seeing someone else.

She remembered one afternoon after school when her father parked in front of the school behind the last bus. Dina started walking to her father when she saw another woman in the car. She was thrilled to see her parents together and thought that things had changed. Her father got out the car, smiled to her, beckoning her toward them. When Dina saw the woman was not her mother, she turned and got on the bus. The next day—her mother's fortieth birthday—her father went to get the ice cream that he said he forgot. He never returned. Dina was always angry after that; angry with her mother; angry with her father for leaving her with her mother; and angry with herself for getting on the bus. It was Rick who helped her rid herself of most of her anger. He helped her become a better person. The truth was that Dina loved Rick.

Dina turned toward the box. She tried to recall whether Rick had ordered anything. Most of his restaurant ordering, he did at the restaurant, and if he wanted anything for himself, he usually asked her to order it for him. She didn't remember ordering anything, answering any kind of ad, or filling out anything in one of her favorite department stores. Who would send her a package? She looked again and saw that it could have been her name on the label if she squinted hard. She untied the cord and tore the brown paper off to expose a plain white box. She took the top off the box and inside, amid gold-color tissue paper, she found a long gray letter envelope. She eased open the flap, lifted the letter, and read the first paragraph.

Congratulations! Dina, you have just won a free all-expenses-paid weekend of fun and renewal at our singles retreat weekend in beautiful West Virginia, where nature abounds. This weekend retreat is guaranteed to give you a new perspective on your life and will fill you with the energy you need to take control of yourself. Make your reservations now by taking a moment to complete the application. Bring a friend if you like. The weekend awaits you. Review the enclosed pamphlet for more information, regulations, and directions to this wonderful opportunity.

"A singles weekend retreat," she said aloud. "But I'm not single. Maybe it would be good to get away, take some time to think."

Dina looked all around the letter, envelope, and box for anything that would tell her who sent the letter, but there was nothing. She'd heard that some companies do random mailings offering cruises and weekends at hotels, all expenses paid. Maybe this was an advertisement. She wondered if the gold tissue paper meant something, but nothing came to mind. She put the letter back in the envelope and took the envelope, along with the brown paper, and put it all back in the box. She took the box to the kitchen to throw it away but placed the box on the brown and beige granite counter instead. She opened the freezer and found a quart of chocolate fudge ice cream, took out a spoon and sat down to gorge—a Dina retreat.

She had just asked her husband of twelve years to move out. What would her mother have to say now? She could just hear her mother's voice. "I told you, you wouldn't be able to keep a man when you're overweight. Look at you now. Instead of taking a long walk, you'd prefer to eat. Look at the huge portion of calorie-laden chocolate fudge. No man wants a woman who doesn't take care of herself. Look at your hair, and speaking of looks, why not do something with the face you inherited from your idiot father? Put on some makeup." Tears rolled down her face again as she tried to tune out her mother's voice in her head. Through her sobs, she took another big spoonful of ice cream and after feeling guilty about eating it, put the quart away.

Dina looked down at herself. She had let herself go. Her hair could use a good trim, and according to her mother's standards, she could drop a pound or two. That wouldn't matter to Rick. He had been so busy with the restaurant lately that he hardly paid attention to her anymore. She turned to look at the box. Nothing on the box gave her any clues about the sender. She'd just toss it. She wasn't single; not yet anyway; and besides, what would she do at a singles retreat?

#

The next day at the nonprofit organization where she worked, she took the letter out and reread it. For some reason she had brought it with her, even though she told herself she would discard it. The ringing of the telephone interrupted her thoughts.

"Hello there, pretty mama."

"Chet, how many times have I asked you not to call me that? It makes me think you're flirting with me. I'm a married woman, remember?" She winced when she said that, thinking that could soon change.

"Well I'm a single man, and I'm not afraid to tell you that you have such a pretty heart," Chet responded in his Alabama accent.

"What do you want, Chet?"

"Just checking to see about that box."

"Box? What box?"

"Didn't you send those pamphlets on?"

"Oh, yes. That box. Yes I shipped the pamphlets yesterday."

"Okay then, honeybunch. Thanks a lot."

Just as she hung up the phone, her supervisor peeped into her office.

"Dina, the committee loved your flyers and promo package. You did a really nice job. Contact the cancer society, and set up a preview. You're getting off to a good start on your new job."

"Thanks, Helen. I sent the pamphlets out already. Chet will receive them soon."

"Good." Helen left.

Dina got out her promo package and flyer to set up a day and time to meet with the cancer society, but she couldn't think about that. What if Rick took her seriously and actually left her? She'd hang out at bars after work like other singles did. Helen would probably expect her to work overtime. She knew she wasn't pretty and she needed to take better care of herself. She had Rick to blame for her weight. He was always bringing home food for her to taste, asking her opinion on the balance of the ingredients, the strength, or subtlety of the taste. Maybe if she took her mother's advice, put on a little makeup, redid her hair, she could be attractive. Yet Chet just told her that she had a pretty heart. Didn't that count for something? Maybe she should go on the singles retreat, just to test the water, so to speak. Just to see if she could be single again. The letter said that she could bring someone with her. She would ask Cary to go with her.

#

"Someone actually sent you a letter to a singles weekend retreat?" Cary said.

Dina looked around the employee room to make sure they were the only two people there. Since it was lunchtime, other employees would be coming in and sitting at their table. Dina wanted to keep this private.

"Here it is." She handed the letter to Cary.

"Who would be so cruel? You don't think it was Ellen, do you?" She took a bite of her egg salad sandwich.

"I don't know, Maybe she and Rick want to run away together."

"Well, good luck to them and good riddance, I say."

Dina didn't respond. She was on the verge of tears and trying desperately to hold strong. The thought of Rick with someone else or even the thought of her without Rick was frightening.

"Dina, it is good riddance, isn't it?"

"I can't believe this is happening. I just never thought he'd run around on me."

"Well, you caught them, didn't you? I mean they were close up on each other." Cary took the letter and put it back in the envelope. "I'll let you be the one to throw it away." She handed the envelope to Dina.

Dina looked at it but didn't take it.

"You are planning to throw it away, aren't you?"

"I'm just so mixed up right now. I don't know what to do." Tears managed to slip out of her eyes and rolled down her face. She swiped them away.

"The thought of her sending you this, so she can be—"

"I don't know that she sent this. I'm just so confused right now. I don't want to say Rick or his waitress sent this. I just need to figure this whole thing out."

"How are you planning to do that?

"Actually, Cary, I thought I would go. I mean I thought we could go."

"We?"

"The letter says I can bring a friend."

"But I'm not ready for that. My divorce was hard. I still love Matt. I'm just not ready for that."

"I think it would be good for both of us. You need to move on. Matt is engaged to someone else, they're planning a wedding, and I need to make a decision about my life."

"And Dina there's another thing. You're…not…single. That seems to be an important part of the weekend."

"But who would know? We just go. I won. I was selected, remember? Someone thinks I'm single. And you are single."

"It's just a weekend, right?" Cary asked.

"We leave Friday evening and return Sunday."

\#

Dina and Cary drove to the singles retreat in West Virginia, about a two-hour drive. The entrance was about a mile off the road and surrounded by woods. In the front and to the right there was a swimming pool and on the other side of it, a tennis court. To the left there was a walking trail with a large poster of wildlife at the entrance. The resort seemed to be a set of five buildings. Dina pulled into the half-full parking lot in front of what was identified as the main building. A sign that said "Singles Retreat Registration" directed the participants to the building. They sat in the car and watched as several men and women went into the building, some with suitcases, while some came out and headed toward the tennis court.

Cary looked at Dina. "Are we really doing this?"

"Yes, now let's get out quickly."

All of the participants were housed in the same building, which held about fifty people. Everyone had a ground-level unit, and Dina and Cary had unit 114, down near the end and close to the tennis court. Their cabin was a plain double-bed room. Dina opened the console and found a TV with a well-stocked bar underneath. The bathroom was strikingly different with its modern granite counter, large shower, extra wide closet and double sinks. In fact, Dina thought she'd stepped into another cabin when she stepped into the bathroom. After they settled in, they went to the dining room where they were told the welcoming address, the Greet and Meet, and then dinner would begin the retreat.

After they were all welcomed, the director, Barbara Fielding, announced that the bar was open and asked everyone to introduce themselves to someone new.

Dina and Cary looked at each other. Cary, without a word, turned around and walked away. She headed out the door and disappeared down the hall. Dina wanted to run after her, but she couldn't move. The thought of having to tell her name, even with a name tag, to each and every person she met and repeat again where she was from and what she did for a living was just too dreadful for her, and she stood, thinking she would escape too.

"Hello, uh Dina?" A tall thin man said, bending down to see her name tag.

"Hello, Walter," Dina said, reading his name tag.

"Do you mind if we just talk a little, I mean if I just talk to you?"

"Talk about what?" She eyed the hallway, searching for Cary.

"I don't care. I just can't go around the room telling my name, and where I work, and where I was born."

Dina smiled. "Were you reading my mind?"

"You, too then, huh?"

Later, Barbara Fielding returned and announced that the dining room was open for seating. The participants seemed to race there. Dina wasn't the only one uncomfortable with the Greet and Meet thing. She took a seat at a table in the middle of the room. Cary returned and took a seat next to her. Dina didn't want to ask Cary what happened to her.

"May I sit here?"

Dina looked up and saw the most gorgeous creature standing with his hand on the back of the chair.

"Please do," she responded. She wished she'd said something else. Please do? What was she thinking? That sounded like she was begging him to sit down. Still, she tried to smile.

The man pulled the seat out and sat next to Dina.

"I'm Dennis," he said holding his name tag in her direction.

She extended her hand. "I'm Dina and this is my friend Cary."

Dennis was easy to talk to since the conversation was mostly about his life, and at this point, Dina needed that. Dennis had a beautiful set of brown eyes, which changed from gray to green as he spoke, and a full head of thick wavy brown hair. She imagined herself playing with his luscious locks when he told her that his wife had passed away from cancer. He spoke with a slight southern accent that she found sexy. He told her that he and his wife met in elementary school, went to the same middle school, and dated all throughout high school and college. During their last year in college, they couldn't wait any longer, and married. They both finished college, and it was when they wanted to start a family that she was diagnosed. He told Dina about how hard it was for him to let her go and how much he loved her. They didn't have children. She had wanted to leave him with a child, to remember her. He had wanted more time with her. Now, he confided with Dina, he wished they'd had a child.

Dina didn't say much. She didn't want to talk about Rick. She thought how lucky Dennis's wife was to have a man who seemed that devoted to her. Rick was devoted to her. She knew it and felt it from him. She was so jealous of every woman who came anywhere near him that she imagined something going on with everyone with whom he came in contact. She accused him unjustly each time. Rick had told her several times that he wanted her; he loved her and only her.

Dennis was a sweet, kind man. He brought her seconds when he got up to get more chicken and rice for himself. He even asked Cary if he could bring her anything. He also brought them both coffee after the meal. Rick would do the same thing. Whenever they visited his parents' house, he always filled her plate and was the one to go back for seconds, for both of them.

#

After dinner, Dennis walked them to their cabin and bid them a good night. When they were inside and in bed, Dina was restless and couldn't sleep. They could hear some of the other singles outside talking and laughing. "Well what do you think?"

"I hope you don't mind, but I'm ready to leave."

"Don't do this. You don't have to meet any one. We're not here for that, remember?

But you should attend some of the sessions tomorrow."

"Well, let's see what they are." Cary sat up and turned on the light. "Oh, look. The first session is: *The Things You and Your Mate Must Have in Common.* Now, how am I to relate to this?"

"Cary, I'm not leaving. I want to stay until the end."

"I've never felt so alone until now. I don't think I'll ever get Matt back."

"Matt is getting married. You should stay, attend the sessions, and just listen. I want to listen and see how this retreat can help me."

The next morning Dina and Cary went to the first session. Dina looked around for Dennis and saw him across the room talking to another woman. She realized that he was doing what she was doing—trying to find herself. The session leader, Walter Cox, held up his bestselling book about the topic and announced that the book would be for sale after the session.

Dina listened to him talk about the need for two people to want to be with each other, have the same relationship goals and the same professional goals. She and Rick had always wanted to be with each other. He was the one who wanted to go to therapy. Rick had always shown her his love for her. They both wanted to move ahead. They had started out in a small apartment in the rough part of town right after college. Then they moved to a larger apartment when he was hired on as the head pastry chef at a big restaurant downtown near the water. They held onto the apartment, and saved for the single-family home they now have. She was recently promoted to project director at her nonprofit organization. Rick encouraged her to apply for the position and she did.

Walter Cox walked across the room and brought her back to his presentation. He said that two people didn't have to have everything in common and gave a simple example of two people choosing different workout routines. Dina realized that Rick got up early and went to the gym almost every morning, but she didn't work out. Rick's going to the gym was all right with her. Did Rick want her to work out? She always thought that as a pastry chef, he had to manage his diet. She never realized that her weight could be a problem for him. She could just hear her mother in that high screechy voice tell her how ugly and fat she was and that no man would want her.

When the session ended, she talked Cary into attending the next session, *How to Find the Person for You.* They took their seats and Cary sat with her arms folded. A man sat down next to Dina and took out a notebook. Dina saw him writing something.

"Jim, I didn't think to bring a notebook with me."

"Hi, Dina," he said, gazing at her name tag. "I always do this. I just take notes."

She should have brought something to write down important things. It could help with her confusion, not to mention that she could take her situation more seriously.

"I saw you in the first session. That was a good session, didn't you think?" Jim asked.

"Yes, it was," she said. Someone noticed her.

"What did you think about the fact that you and your partner should have things in common?" Jim asked.

"I never considered that," Dina said.

"It is true," Jim said.

"I try to understand my boyfriend, isn't that enough?" Dina asked. She hated to lie.

"I always thought that if I made enough money for my wife and me and if I got promotions then my wife would move up with me. We started out small, and later, we moved into a larger place. We were married for fifteen years, and for all those years, I was happy and proud of myself that I could take care of my family. When we had our four children, I worked even harder to provide for them. Then one day, she told me she was never happy, that she'd always felt something was missing. She said I was selfish and she walked out."

"I'm sorry that happened to you. I think my h, my boyfriend is seeing someone else." She didn't know why she told him that. It could make him feel better about his situation.

He cast his eyes down. "She was, too."

"What happened when you tried talking to her?"

"Not much. She said it was too late."

The session leader, Dr. Elizabeth Freeman, began her presentation. She talked about how important it was to have the right frame of mind to find the person for you. She talked about positive thinking or thinking about yourself in a positive manner and having a positive mindset about the opposite sex. Her mother came to her mind again, and she heard her mother demean her father. "Don't be so stupid," she would say to her father. One time she said to Dina, "Is the idiot home yet?" Dina realized that she spoke about Rick the same way. After they were married, she remembered calling him stupid when he did something he thought was fun. It drove her crazy when Rick walked out of the house after she spoke to him like that. She thought about her father walking away. The last time she called him stupid, Rick was gone all afternoon, and when she came to her senses, she went to the restaurant to try to apologize to him. She promised herself that she would never do that again. She had. Recently, she called him a pig. Against her promise, she had turned into her mother.

Dr. Freeman also talked about keeping yourself "open" and Dina eyed Cary as she uncrossed her arms.

"Not only do you have to keep yourself open, but make yourself friendly as well. Who wants to meet someone grumpy?" Dr. Freeman went on to say. Dina was filled with anger for a long while and sometimes when she and Rick argued, her anger would gush out of her, a dam breaking. Rick would stop her and say, "I'm not the cause of all that." Over the years, her anger began to diminish.

After lunch, Dina didn't go back to the cabin during rest time. She went to the large game room where she saw many participants playing pool, checkers, talking, or reading. She found a seat over by the bookcase and near the window, and sat down to think. She recalled the conversations from the men she happened to sit next to and the discussions from the sessions that filled her mind with questions about her marriage, questions about herself.

The evening's session was on *Being Single in Today's Time and The Economy*. Dr. Mary Short led the session about the pros and cons of singlehood today. She asked the participants to ask questions of her. Several people nodded when one woman asked her to define "singlehood," because most people today thought that if you were dating, you were no longer single even if you were not living together. Many of the older participants didn't understand that way of thinking, "especially since there were no perks to accompany this situation," an older man said. Many people laughed, and he smiled, turning around in all directions.

Dina began to think of herself without Rick. She didn't think she could do be without him. From the time they met, he was her best friend. She would have to share her thoughts with someone else. She wouldn't sit by the window and wait for him to come from work, or listen to his funny stories about things that happened at the restaurant, or sit with him on their porch that he designed for them. Rick would not be there to help her move furniture around or surprise her with his special gifts, and Rick would never fix the pipe under the kitchen sink. She thought about Rick and the house. He was the one who wanted the house. It was in need of work and he promised her he would fix it up.

#

The next day, after the morning's session, she and Cary packed up to leave.

"Let's get the hell out of here," Cary said, getting in the car.

"You didn't get anything out of this weekend?"

"Yes I did. I want Matt back and I know just what I'm going to do to get him back."

Dina didn't want to be like Cary, stuck in a world that wasn't hers.

"Cary, he's engaged to someone else. They have plans to marry."

"I don't know if I should tell you this or not, but I called him. I called him this weekend and talked to him."

"Why would you do that? What did he say?" She tried not to sound disappointed, but she felt sorry for Cary.

"He said he was glad to hear from me and know that I'm doing fine, and he doesn't want any hard feelings between us, and he understood what I meant when I said I wanted more."

"That doesn't sound like he wants to leave his fiancé."

Cary spent the rest of the drive crying and being sorry that she demanded too much from Matt and drove him away.

After they arrived home, Dina turned on her cell phone and noticed that Rick had called her eight times over the weekend. He left five messages asking her if he could come and talk. She saw from the dried eggs and bacon on a plate left in the sink that Rick had come home.

Home.

Rick was home.

The weekend made her see that she had some things she needed to work on if she wanted her marriage to work. She had vowed that she would never treat Rick the way her mother treated her father, yet she had done the same thing to him. She realized that Rick had made her happy. He treated her better than she treated him. Dina sometimes wondered why he loved her, why he put up with her abuse. One day she'd asked him and he told her that when she was kind to him, she was better than any woman he'd ever met. She wanted to be a better person one hundred percent of the time with Rick. She wanted to save her marriage, but first she needed to save herself.

She went to the kitchen and dialed the number of the restaurant. While waiting, she opened the freezer to take out the chocolate fudge ice cream. She thought for a minute, put it back, and closed the freezer door.

"Hello, Rick?"

The box with the letter was still on the counter.

"Hi, sweetheart. Are you all right? I've been worried about you."

"I'm home and I'm sorry, Rick. I'm sorry. I don't want you to leave. I love you. Let's go to couple's therapy.

She pulled the letter out of the box and held it in her hand. Fortuitous or Arranged?

FRAGILE

S. G. Basu

The box arrived the day Superstorm Annie was set to hit Gantor City. It was not just any box, but one as wide as the Volvo, and almost as tall. It was one gigantic specimen, the king of all boxes, the biggest Tori had seen in a while.

Tori had taken the day off, prepping like crazy for the storm. She had to; she was alone with the kids. Tori was a little scared. Not that she had never been on her own before, but dire predictions of the superstorm blasting nonstop on the airwaves had made her nervous. So she had gone on a buying spree—bread, potatoes, rice, lots and lots of packaged water, flashlights, batteries, ranger boots, and more. Tori had hoped to be done with the shopping by midday, but one short trip stretched into a half-day-long stuff-hunting expedition. There were long queues everywhere she went—at the grocery shops, at the fueling pump, at the wholesaler's. People seemed to be preparing for Armageddon. Tori shamelessly did her part, relieved only when she had secured double the bare necessities. She was feeling quite proud of her capabilities as she made the trip back home. And then, as soon as she approached the driveway, she saw the box.

"Whoa, Mom! What's that?" Mirka yelled from the back seat. That girl had eyes.

"Yeah, what's that, Mom?" the older and quieter Lawrence joined in.

"I've no idea," Tori replied, cursing under her breath. "What the hell?"

The box took up more than half the width of the driveway, Tori noted as she pulled in, stopping halfway through. Goddammit, not enough room to scrape past.

"How do we get the SUV in, Mom?" Mirka chirped again.

"Let me think, okay?" Tori snapped. Her daughter was only trying to help; Tori knew that, but her head was on fire. Must be something that idiot, Sammy, had ordered. Stupid guy. Not just away partying while the storm was about to hit, he also had to order some blasted thing.

"What did you order, Mommy?"

"Will you please be quiet, Lawrence?" Tori yelled. "Both of you, quiet."

Tori rested her forehead on the steering wheel. It did not matter who ordered that box, something had to be done about it. But how long did they have? Her hand reached for the radio button. "This is Weather Station KWS20 reporting on Superstorm Annie. A hurricane warning is in effect for townships twenty-one, twenty-four, thirty-four, thirty-five, fifty-four, and sixty-seven. This includes the greater Gantor City area to Puffin Bay. Sustained winds of one hundred fifty miles per hour and greater expected. Twenty inches of precipitation is likely in the next twenty-four hours. Annie is estimated to hit the listening area in the next fifty-five minutes."

Tori slapped the button off. She had about an hour—to either unpack and retrieve whatever was inside the box, or find a place to store that darned box together with whatever was inside it, allowing her to get her vehicle inside the garage.

"Okay, move it," she said, spinning around to let six-year-old Mirka and ten-year-old Lawrence out of their safety buckets.

The duo made a beeline for the box. It was a perfect cube, sides almost as tall as Tori. The label was useless—parts of it were covered with blotches, and sections of it had been peeled off. The only thing Tori could make out was it was indeed addressed to her and it was from Lo-Mart.

"That's what happens when you keep cutting costs," Tori grumbled. "Can't even stick a label on properly anymore."

What did Sammy get from Lo-Mart, she wondered? The surface gave Tori no clues.

"Mommy, look here," Mirka squealed from behind the box's ample girth. "It says FRA-JEE-LEE."

"Fragile," Lawrence corrected.

Fragile? The gears in Tori's brain spun furiously. What could Sammy need from Lo-Mart that's fragile? Not need, she corrected herself. Want. Something impractical obviously. Sammy always found stuff to buy. As if they didn't have enough junk already.

Tori put her shoulder against the box and pushed a little. It did not budge an inch. How was she going to move this? She looked around. No neighbors to be seen—everyone must be out doing last-minute stuff-hunting of course. A drop of water landed on Tori's cheek, making her frown.

"You two, let's get inside. The storm's coming soon."

Shooing the children into the house, Tori got back into the Volvo. She had to get it into the garage. Easier said than done, given the way the box was blocking the driveway. But leaving the vehicle outside in the storm was not an option so...

For what felt like forever, Tori steered the Volvo forward and backward, over and over again. Slowly she got the front of the automobile in, then a bit of the body, and then somehow she managed to get its wide backside into the safety of the garage. More irritated than tired, she walked around the Volvo, shaking her head at the scrape on the fender caused by the maneuvering. She patted the vehicle affectionately, as if in apology.

"Well, at least I got you in," she muttered.

With a tiny sigh, Tori pulled herself away and opened the trunk. The precious supplies she had gathered over the better part of the day had to be stowed away. Once that was over, she started off to take some measurements of the box.

The grim conclusions started streaming in right away. There was no room in the garage to store this. It was too large to fit through the front door, so that was not an option either. Where else could she put it?

Tori slapped her head. Why was she even thinking of moving it? The damn box was too heavy to haul around anyway. She would have to open it up and then get the contents indoors. Tori tested at the reinforced belt that encircled the body of the box—too rigid for her to get through within an hour. Then there was ripping the box itself, a triple-walled corrugated box, no less.

The shipping label was a shoddy job, but they had paid good attention to the packaging. Too much attention almost. The entire box was crisscrossed with a pale blue tape, certainly the heavy duty Dino brand polymer-tape, the color indicating its wilderness-grade strength. Like it had a missile inside or a priceless heirloom or as if the packers knew it had to brave Superstorm Annie. Whatever the reason, the box was not intended to be opened quickly. Cutting through all that tape and industrial grade packaging? It would be quite impossible to—

"Mommiee!"

"Yes, Mirka."

"My tummy's making funny sounds. Lawrence thinks I'm hungry."

Tori chucked the tape measure into one of Sammy's toolboxes and headed inside. Not one moment of slack around this house—prep for survival, solve the riddle of mystery boxes, and then provide for the family too.

What did Sammy order? The question buzzed on as Tori warmed up dinner. The only thing they went looking for recently was the filter for the furnace. A filter that was as big as Tori's arm, not half the driveway. Unless Sammy ordered a thousand of them. Anyway, they had found no filters at Lo-Mart. Sammy and Tori had simply strolled around the toy aisle, the home section, and finally the entertainment department. Just browsing.

"Mom, when's Dad-dad coming back?" Mirka asked.

"Not anytime soon, Mirka," Tori replied, trying her best to keep the gruffness in her voice from showing.

"Will he be late because of the storm?" Mirka mumbled in between mouthfuls of battered rice cakes.

"Maybe." Tori had not checked. She was far too annoyed with Sammy and busy with her own troubles to keep track of his daily whereabouts. She did not feel the need to—the guy was out partying with his friends anyway.

"He could've moved the box easy," Lawrence declared.

"But he's not here, is he?" Tori reminded as gently as she could, even though she itched to slam her fist down on the table and end the babble. "So it's up to us to figure out what to do with it."

"Maybe we could call the firehouse," Mirka suggested.

This chatter was not going to end. Tori breathed in deep to collect herself.

Lawrence rolled his eyes and chuckled. "And ask them to move a box for us? Firehouse people have other...more important stuff to do."

"We could see if Mr. Jones is around," Mirka said next, thinking of their friendliest neighbor.

Tori suppressed a smile. The sweet Mr. Jones was pushing ninety and was not exactly an ideal candidate for lifting weights or cutting through Dino tape. "Um, might be a bit too heavy for him," she said.

"What's inside the box, Mom?"

"I don't know, Mirka."

"It's Dad-dad's stuff, right? Could be the telescope he wanted to get?" Lawrence pondered, absentmindedly stirring his soup.

Tori sighed. Another one of Sammy's mess-producing, junk-accumulating hobbies. Stargazing, he called it. It had started two years ago, when Mirka was four and Lawrence had been curious about a meteor shower. In came the charts and scopes, eyepieces, binoculars, and whatnot. Sammy, along with the kids, had set up the northern balcony with the stuff—they called it the observation deck—and the rest of the house became their starship. To this day, Lawrence and Mirka called their home Starship Pathbreaker 876, a twist on the address 876 Broken Path Drive. Sammy had a way of rallying the forces, of getting the kids inspired, Tori had to admit. He was always a fun, excitable kind of guy, the life of the party, the eternal charmer.

"Mom? Could it be the telescope?"

"It's too large to be a regular telescope, Lawrence. Unless you guys decided to turn the house into a real observatory."

Lawrence and Mirka erupted in a cascade of giggles. Tori did not want to join in but did anyway. The kids' laughter always melted her anger away. Not for long enough though. It always, always surged right back.

It was an ongoing battle, keeping the house, or even just a bit of the house, to herself and in a state of her kind of Zen, like Tori wished. It seemed like a lifetime ago that Tori's abode was a meticulously curated slice of nirvana. Working as a coroner's assistant had taken a daily toll on Tori's sanity, but the moment she stepped inside the house, peace had refreshed her soul and made her ready for anything life could throw at her. Tori needed that peace. She existed because of that peace. Tori's favorite spot was the meditation room—the vaulted roof, the twelve-foot glass wall that overlooked the protected grasslands behind the house, the reclaimed stone floor. It was the last project Tori had worked on with her dad before he was diagnosed with advanced pancreatic cancer. It was a treasure, Tori's piece of happiness.

Then Sammy had happened.

"The kitchen windows are nice and big, Mom," Lawrence said, grinning impishly. "Perfect place for another telescope, don't you think?"

"Yes, why not," Tori replied. "The house is all yours."

"You have the White Room, Mom," Mirka said, rattling off words she had picked up from her father. That was Sammy's line of defense, always, reminding Tori of her meditation room. "We never get in *there*."

"Thank goodness, I do," Tori replied, dumping the dishes in the sink. She stole a glance at the clock—not much time left to decide on the box.

Sammy...Tori's thoughts slipped back twelve years, like they did so often.

Sammy was a whirlwind. If Tori was obsessive about organizing, Sammy was the embodiment of free spirit. His liveliness had claimed Tori quickly—she fell prey easier than she would have if she had not been reeling from her father's death. It was not until Mirka was born that Tori realized how her life had changed, for better and for worse. Sure, Sammy had filled her life to the brim again, but it was a life that had little predictability and almost no structure. Everything was a rush, everything a deluge of spontaneity. It had felt good for a bit, but it had grown too overwhelming with time.

"We can't get the box inside, but we could try to open it up on the driveway," Tori declared, setting her reminiscing aside. Now was time to get this done. "I'll have to get the tools. You guys can watch TV."

"Why can't we come outside and help you?" Mirka asked.

Because you wouldn't be of any real help, Tori thought. At least if they stayed inside she would not have to mind them while unwrapping that thing.

"Dad-dad always lets us help," Lawrence joined in.

The kids belonged to their father. Not like they were not Tori's but they were more Sammy's than hers. The three were tight. Like Tori had always been with her father. After the kids grew up some more, there would be no wresting control of the house from Sammy. He had his minions— eager to give into whims, joining forces to set up a drum-pad set or cook up coq au vin from scratch.

"Okay, come on out," Tori gave in grudgingly.

The trio headed out of the house, Mirka and Lawrence marching ahead. The wind had picked up some more; it blew Tori's hair around and stung her face.

"This is cool," Mirka yelled, twirling around a couple of times. "A project with Mommy."

Even the six-year-old was a confident apprentice to Sammy. Their last project had included "repurposing" the family room. Under Sammy's carefree guidance, they had installed a 3-D entertainment system, complete with educational games. Sammy said it was the latest technology—never mind the house-shaking, headache-inducing sound those gigantic speakers made.

Speakers! The thought ripped through Tori, stunning her for a bit. She calmed down in a flash, as people often do after a lifetime of handling kids. That has to be it, Tori concluded, the speakers. They had seen the set right after they had walked past the home decor at Lo-Mart, past the Claudette floor vase.

That vase, Tori remembered lovingly. Such a beauty it was; its slender neck soaring, its bulging translucent girth shimmering with the vivid colors of the tropical oceans. Tori had not seen such meticulous cutouts in stoneware ever before. That Claudette was perfection. It was made for her White Room.

"Look at the price, Tori," Sammy had said after looking at the tag.

Claudettes always were expensive; there was nothing new about that.

"It'll be perfect next to the furnace." Tori had traced the cool, sensuous curves of the grand Claudette.

"Don't you want to take the kids to Disneyland this year?"

Sure, she did. But the vase was just...She sighed. "Okay, let's get out of here."

"Sorry. You know we're maxed out after the remodeling."

Like she was enjoying the fruits of that.

"Dad." Lawrence had appeared, delight making his little voice tremble. "They have our speakers."

"They do?"

"And their box says six hundred fifty," his sister had shrieked, jumping up and down like the Energizer Bunny.

In a second, the threesome had bounded away, leaving Tori alone and pining for the Claudette.

She had found them later, huddled together in front of a pair of towering silver boxes generating noise.

"Look, Tori, what they have in stock today. Just the specs I was looking for too."

A sidelong glance at the price tag had come naturally. "Thought we were planning to save up for Disneyland." Tori knew she had sounded bitter.

"Yeah. It's a good sale though," he had mumbled, dragging himself away from the display.

They had all been quiet on the way back home.

The howling of the wind and the slight tremor that spread through the house brought Tori back to the present. The cheek! Sammy had bought those confounded speakers after all, but he'd denied her that perfect Claudette.

"Mommieee!" Mirka was waving her arms frantically to grab Tori's attention. "What do we do?"

Tori knew exactly what to do. There was no way she was risking her back trying to haul that box. She was not going to battle the packaging either. The speakers could go to hell. But she still had to deal with Sammy's minions, convince them somehow of the soundness of her resolution.

"I think we should cover it up with tarp and leave it here."

"Leave it outside? In the storm?" Lawrence made a Sammy face, one that screamed, *have you lost your mind?*

Tori inhaled, hoping the breath would help her keep it together. Why was there so much of Sammy and so little of her in the kids?

"I'm not sure we could unpack the thing in the time we have. We have less than a half hour until the storm hits. And you see the package. The seals are pretty tough."

"What if the wind blows it away?"

"Well, it's quite heavy. It'll most likely hold its ground."

"Can't just leave it outside all alone in the storm." Mirka raised a squeaky voice of protest.

"Guys, even if we could open the box up, I don't think the three of us could move what's inside of it."

A chorus rose: "What's inside of it?"

"I think the box has your dad's speakers. Those giant ones you were checking out at Lo-Mart the other day."

"Really? Cool," Mirka chirped.

"Okay. So, who's gonna help me make a good and strong tent of tarp over it?"

Within minutes, they were wrapping and tying and securing the prized box with the speakers that Dad-dad had ordered. "Poor Dad-dad, poor speakers." "Would've been so much fun if he were here." "How many days till he gets back, Mom?" It went on and on and on, an endless lament for their missing comrade. By the time Tori was done building and securing the makeshift cover over the box, she was exhausted in every way. The sky had started to give way to nature's wrath.

#

The phone buzzed with all its might a little after the kids had finally gone to sleep. The ring sounded like an alarm in Tori's tired brain, making her jump.

"T-," Sammy's voice drifted in from the other end in unsteady spurts. "All okay?"

"Yes."

"I've b-n calling you since noon. Couldn't g-t through."

"The phone lines are messed up here. The storm's coming in."

"I'm s- sorry. The timing turned out so awful."

Tori swallowed the lump of hurt and forced a chuckle.

"That's all right, Sammy. This is a chance of a lifetime. You would have been a fool to pass it up." Tori repeated the words Sammy had told her a week ago when he was offered the free tickets to the Terra Copa finals. The storm had been predicted then, although its course was not set in stone. He yearned to go, she had figured that much. Tori was not one to stand in anyone's way, never had been wired that way. But she had wished for him to stay. Be there for her, with her.

"Should've refused them," Sammy said.

Silence swooped in on the conversation; Tori did not want to look too hard for a reply.

"Tori, you there?" Sammy's always-vibrant voice was a bit gloomy, or maybe it was her imagination, Tori thought. Sammy did not do regrets; he did not have time for such things. "Did Lo-Mart call you? They're supposed to—"

"They didn't call me, but there's a box for you." So he had known about the delivery and had not even cared to tell her.

"What? Already? It wasn't supposed to get there before the weekend."

"Well, it has."

"Do you like it?" Sammy ventured after a hesitant pause.

"Like it?"

Tori wanted to say many things. How the heck did he expect her to like some effing speakers? How did he expect to justify the expense? Especially after he snuck behind her back to get them? And now Tori had to think about keeping them safe. She did not say much. She walked over to the liquor cabinet instead and yanked the door open.

"I don't even know what it is, Sammy. How can I like it?"

"You didn't? You didn't open the box?"

"I couldn't cut through the packaging. It was too tough. I didn't have enough time."

"Can't believe they messed up the delivery. Wanted to surprise you. Hold on—where did you store the box?"

"It's on the driveway."

"You d-didn't leave it out-s-de?" His voice was breaking up. But not fast enough. Tori reached for the bottle of *Ruined*

Woman. She needed a few shots tonight. *Unbelievable!* He expected her to break her back getting that box inside?

"I covered it up well, Sammy. It should be safe enough. Hooked it up to the wall too."

"It's out in the storm?" Sammy yelled. Tori was sure that if she could reach him, she would have clobbered his head right now. "The C-dette is out i- the st-m?"

"W-what did you say? Can't hear you, Sammy."

"Can't h-r y-u, Tori."

"Sammy?"

"S- y safe, o-y. I'll try t-"

The traces of his voice faded away. Tori sat, not breathing, phone on her lap. Disoriented moments slipped past. Until she sat up with a start and tried to dial his number. Again and again. All the calls froze somewhere out there, in between the soaked earth and the raging storm-gods up in the sky.

C-dette? Did Sammy mean Claudette? Did he order the Claudette for her from Lo-Mart? It could not be, Tori tried to convince herself. There was a time when Sammy would have, but not now, not anymore.

A gust of wind crashed against the long, rain-drenched glass windows of the kitchen, making them rattle.

Tori slipped the phone into her pocket, grabbed the bottle of *Ruined Woman,* and strode to the windows overlooking the driveway. Outside, the winds were wild, the trees danced to their ruthless rhythm, and the box held its ground. How long it could endure, Tori did not know, but she vowed to keep it company through the dismal night.

She pulled up a chair and began her watch.

SOUNDS LIKE TEEN SPIRIT

Spencer Stephens

Pittsburgh, Pennsylvania
September 1991

Maximo's mouth was so dry with anxiety that his father had to lick the flap on the overfull envelope. Then the boy sat on a rocker on his screened-in front porch and waited for almost two hours so he could make sure that the postman actually picked it up.

When the postal truck turned the corner onto his street, Maximo stood up and stared, fearful that the mailman might skip his house or that the envelope might slip from the man's hand before it could be pulled into the mail truck. Once he saw the packet tossed into an on-board mail sack, Maximo slumped with exhaustion.

The mailman leaned out his window. "Hey, do you need help? Are you okay?"

Maximo held one hand on his heart and held a palm aloft, just like Father Pete at Our Lady of Sorrows did when he was beseeching God. "Please make sure that envelope gets to South Bend, Indiana," he said. "If I don't get into Notre Dame, my life is literally, like, over."

Maximo took comfort because the man looked sympathetic, like he'd seen this sort of thing before. As the mailman smiled, waved, and motored away, Maximo thought he could read the man's lips and that he said, "Well, I wish you good luck." But what he really said was, "You are a wing nut."

For the next few months, Maximo imagined dozens of creative ways that his application to Notre Dame might have been lost, destroyed, or ignored. One night at the dinner table, he interrupted his father, who was excited because he'd just gotten a raise. "Dad, could you call the admissions office at Notre Dame and double-check for me that they have my references and my transcript?"

His father wrinkled his chin. "Max, I called a few weeks ago. They have it. You were right there with me when I talked to them."

"I know, but it seems like we should have heard by now. Maybe something happened. Maybe they lost part of my stuff. Or maybe some of my papers got mixed in with somebody else's or maybe they got misfiled. I heard that at NYU, a janitor tossed out a whole box full of applications and nobody realized for weeks. Can you call again just to make sure? Dad, it's just a phone call. It's just—"

Maximo's father held up a hand and cut him off. "If it's so important, why don't you call?"

"A high school kid can't just call up the admissions office. They would think I was desperate or weird. Can you call them? *Please, Dad?*"

His father took a handful of Maximo's black hair and shook gently. "Will you calm down already? They told me they have all your paperwork. It's there. They have it. Your grades and your scores are excellent. I have no doubt you're going to get in. Plus, you sent applications to plenty of other schools. You'll get into one of them, too. Notre Dame is not the only school on the planet. Now eat your dinner."

"Dad, please. I have to get into Notre Dame. I have to. There would be no point in even going to college if I didn't." Maximo's throat had tightened and his voice sounded like a squeaky party balloon losing air. He didn't notice the parental glances exchanged right in front of him and didn't sense his parents' fear that he had become obsessive. Maximo talked often to his parents about his fascination with Joe Montana, who may have been Notre Dame's most famous alum, but that didn't seem to explain how completely absorbed the boy had become with a school he had visited once for ninety minutes on a frigid morning eight months ago.

His parents might not have fretted had Maximo disclosed that he had become captivated by Mary Bravura, the girl genius in his AP calculus class who changed the color of every room she entered. Whenever she glanced in Maximo's direction with her green eyes, his tongue dissolved into a tasteless pudding. Her father was a wealthy Notre Dame alum who had a campus building named after him, so she knew far in advance where she would be attending college. Twice, Maximo had approached her intending to start a conversation. Both times, sudden bladder pressure forced him to flee to the boys' room before he could utter a syllable.

Maximo knew that he and Mary would finally connect once they got to Notre Dame. He had it all planned out. Feeling and looking self-reliant, Maximo would be in the coffee shop at Hesburgh Library, engrossed in a copy of *Love in the Time of Cholera*. Mary would step in for an espresso and would recognize him. The sight of a studious and independent boy whose reading material revealed that he was a true romantic would make her regret that she had not once spoken to him during four whole years of high school. She would sit down next to him and apologize for interrupting his reading. Her polite approach would leave Maximo feeling cool and in control. He would be thoughtful and witty and would make her laugh. She would touch him on the hand.

They would become the kind of lovers who read poems to one another while they picnicked.

Notre Dame, Maximo thought. *I have to get into Notre Dame.* He stared at the macaroni salad and fried cod on his dinner plate.

His father slapped the table, which made Maximo regain his focus. "Holy Mother of God, will you stop talking like that? You're driving everybody in this house crazy, especially me. Your life will be just fine no matter what college you go to."

#

On a December day when the clouds were dense, Maximo and his pals talked during study hall about how it would be when they started getting letters back from colleges. "My mother used to work in the admissions office at Ohio State. She says that if the envelope they send you is stuffed full of paper, it means you're in," Alejandro said. "If it's thin, it's just a one-pager that says *Sorry, loser.*"

"That's not always true," Dylan said, chewing on a drinking straw. "My cousin got into every school he applied to and most of the envelopes he got were thin."

"Wait. Are you saying he applied to Notre Dame?" Maximo asked.

"No. I never said that. He only applied to junior colleges that take almost everybody. He knew he could never get into

Notre Dame. When he was in high school, all he did was smoke weed and his grades sucked."

"What the hell? Dude, that's a stupid thing to say. Junior college is way different from a real college and not even in the same galaxy as Notre Dame. Why would you even go there?"

"Will you lighten up? I was just saying, that's all."

That night, Maximo dreamt that a thin envelope from Notre Dame had come in the mail while he was at school. He wanted to run all the way home so he could open it, only in his dream, his feet were moving really fast but he wasn't going anywhere. Then his principal tackled him and gave him detention because he had left school early. Maximo had to sit alone in a big room on a wooden chair. The fluorescent lights made a hum that was driving him slowly, slowly insane and he was wearing only his underpants, which at first was not a problem except that they kept getting smaller and smaller, leaving him more and more exposed and the chair was cold against his skin. Then a sharp-dressed man who he remembered from Notre Dame walked past the door to the classroom where Maximo was sitting. The man shook his head and squinted as he assessed the nearly naked Maximo. Maximo shouted after him, "No, there's been a mistake. It's a mistake. This is only a dream." The man kept walking on his way to meet with a different kid—some guy who was a lousy student, who wasn't even Catholic but was a really good inside linebacker and who was going to play football for Notre Dame.

Maximo woke up in the dark seeing blinking spots and had to remind himself to start breathing. He got out of bed and stomped around his room, panting, and he slammed his palm against the wall right next to the poster of Joe Montana wearing his Notre Dame football uniform. "Why haven't I heard from them already? I can't stand all this waiting."

Heavy footsteps approached in the hall. His father skidded into Maximo's doorway, wearing just his pajama bottoms, his eyes wide. "Are you okay?"

"Dad, what if I don't get into Notre Dame? What am I going to do? I've never wanted anything so bad in my whole entire life."

Maximo's father gave the boy a playful shove, and he flopped backward onto his bed. "You're *unbelievable*. Go back to sleep."

After his father left the room, Maximo kneeled at his bedside and prayed the rosary, hoping to calm himself.

#

One Saturday, Maximo and his little brother were in the basement playing guitars when Maximo's mother yelled from upstairs, "Maxie, a letter came for you from Notre Dame." In three strides, he cleared the thirteen basement stairs and then slid on his socks into the kitchen where his mother held a parchment envelope. In the space for the return address, in embossed script, the kind he had seen on framed documents, it said University of Notre Dame. Max opened his hands to receive the envelope, the same way he did at mass whenever Father Pete placed a communion wafer in his palm. His head felt light and the tips of his fingers felt as if they might be part of someone else's hands. He became afraid that he might lose control of his hands and that they would tear the letter into pieces. The thought of this made his stomach feel empty and far away and like it might stay that way forever. He held the envelope up to the light, looking in vain for clues. His mother took it. "Let me have it already. I'll open it."

Maximo snatched it back. "It's *mine*." He dug his finger under the flap and the perfect paper began to tear. He opened the letter and silently read: "The Committee on Admissions has completed evaluation of your application for admission. I am pleased to report that your academic achievements and personal qualities have earned you a place in our incoming freshman class."

Maximo inhaled, deeply, slowly and smoothly, something he hadn't done in months. Water came to his eyes. "This is unbelievable," he said. He touched away his tears with a fingertip.

"Oh, no," his mother said. "Is it bad news?" She pulled all ten of her fingers into a ball and guarded her chin. "Don't be upset, honey. Sometimes these things are a blessing in disguise."

Maximo took his hand away from his face and made an easy motion. He imagined he was smoothing a dry eraser across a white board. "Just relax, Mom," he said. "It's all good. They even gave me a scholarship that will cover almost all of the tuition." Maximo slid to the floor and scanned the letter again. "This is, like, so golden." Life at Notre Dame flashed before his eyes: moving into a dorm and chatting happily with his new classmates, all of them looking peacefully entitled to their places; walking into unfamiliar classrooms that smelled of fresh paper and Pine-Sol. He would burrow a place for himself, and he would *belong*. He would call out professors for missing the nuances that were the essence of Hemingway. He would spice his conversations with droll allusions to Shakespeare's comedies. People would seek him out for his seminal knowledge of bands from the 1960s. He would be the version of himself he had always imagined he could be: grounded, knowledgeable, eternally pleasant, a bottomless well of serenity.

His mother kneeled down and kissed him. "Sweetie, *you got in*. You must be so excited. This is everything you've been hoping for. You got into Notre Dame." She wiggled and squealed and kissed him again. "We've got to call your father right now." She grabbed the phone and began punching buttons. "He'll be pleased as punch. Oh, this is so wonderful. I'm so proud of you. I can't wait for you to tell Mrs. Townsend at the guidance office. She's just going to pop when she hears."

Maximo reached over and hung up on his the call. "*Mother*," he said. "Just take it easy, okay? Just calm down. Can we please not make a big deal out of this?"

THE EYES HAVE IT

Joseph Radko Jr.

Usually I love to get boxes in the mail because I like getting things. But I've become more cautious because the last package that arrived still sticks in my mind. It's the only time a box ever ran away from me.

I found the box on the white wooden table in the kitchen when I got home from class. I turned it over looking for the name of the recipient.

"Whose box?" Steve, my rangy brown-haired housemate asked.

"Doesn't have a name on it," I said as I turned it back over.

"I know that," Steve said. "I found it on the doorstep and brought it in."

Suddenly, the box started shaking in my hands. Before I could put it down, the lid popped open and two pink tentacles shot out of the box and grabbed me. Then a large green eye popped up and peered at me. As I gulped, the tentacles released me, the thing gave a high-pitched squeal as it fell back into the box, and it scuttled away on two tentacles that emerged from the bottom of the box.

I shook my head. Was I dreaming? Or had a creature the size of a large cat but consisting solely of a big green eye and four tentacles, like a starfish on steroids, just run from the room?

"Hey, Josh, what the hell was that?" Steve asked, staring at the kitchen door the errant package had exited through.

He looked pale and shaky. I guess I hadn't dreamed it.

"I don't know," I said. "Let's go find it."

"You want to go look for that thing?" Steve said, staring at me. "Are you out of your mind?"

I wasn't known for my courage, but this thing was too cool to let get away.

"It's just an exotic animal of some type." Right? It had to be. "It's probably terrified. We have to help it."

I hurried in the direction the creature had scampered. Steve followed. A whimper escaped from under the couch in the living room. I pulled up the slipcover and the big green eye looked out at me. Somehow the Eye had squeezed the box between the back of the sofa and the wall. It squealed again and retreated back into the box and shut its cover.

Steve was still staring, dumbfounded.

"Maybe it's a dog or something," he suggested.

"Did you order a really weird-looking dog recently?" I asked.

He shook his head.

"Whatever it is, it's scared of us," I said. "Let's coax it out."

"You'd think that it would be used to scaring people," Steve said, "considering it only has one bizarre eye."

As if the creature had understood him, the box bolted out from behind the couch, heading for the stairs. I grabbed at it but couldn't hold on. The thing inside was strong for its size. It ran over me, up our stairs, and into the second-floor bathroom.

"I think you hurt its feelings," I told Steve.

Our housemate Sherry came running down the stairs.

"A box with legs just ran into the bathroom!"

"Freaky, isn't it?" Steve said. "It just came in the mail."

Sherry looked at both of us incredulously, then sighed.

"Some creature comes in the mail and all you two can do is stand around?" Sherry said.

"I tried to catch it, and it knocked me down," I said as I got up off the floor.

"I'll bet you Leah ordered it," Steve said, "as part of her marine biology major."

"Where is Leah anyway?" Sherry said.

A scream from the upstairs bathroom solved that mystery.

"Oh my God!" Leah shouted as she stormed downstairs. "What is that thing?"

"Somehow I don't think Leah ordered it," Sherry said.

"It has tentacles so it must be a squid or octopus," I said, still trying to convince myself we hadn't just entered Crazy Town.

"It's not a squid or octopus," Leah argued. "I felt one of its tentacles as I slipped past it, and it had no suckers."

All three of us stared at her for a moment in surprise.

"I'm a scuba diver, remember?" she said. "I've seen squid and octopi, and that was neither. Now who's going to get that thing out of the bathroom?"

There were no volunteers.

I'd lost my courage after being trampled by the thing. It was strong.

"Okay," Leah said, glaring at Steve and I suspiciously. "Let's start at the beginning. How did this creature get here, and why is it in our bathroom?"

Crud. If I explained that I had let the Eye out of the box, they might all insist that I go after it.

"Steve insulted the Eye," I said instead, pointing at him as a preemptive strike, "and it ran in there."

"Well, you let the Eye out!" Steve pointed back at me.

"You named it?" Sherry asked at the same moment.

"Yes, I named it," I said. "It's a living being. It deserves a name."

"Fine," Leah said. "You like it so much, you deal with it."

Crud again.

"Maybe we should call somebody," I suggested, "like animal control or something?"

"No animal control," Leah said. "That will take too long. Someone," she added in a tone that left no chance that it would be her, "needs to go up there and face it! We need our bathroom back. I have a date and my dress and makeup are in there."

The three of us stared at her again.

"Okay, there's something weird in the bathroom," Leah said. "But life goes on, and my life includes a party tonight, so that thing has to be moved elsewhere. If it needs a bathroom, put it in your bathroom down here."

There are these times in life when everyone looks to you so that they don't have to do it themselves. I hate those times.

"Josh you were the one who opened the box," Steve said, staring me down, "so you should take care of it."

They all glared at me as if I had created the Eye or something.

"Traitor," I said to him.

"Say hello to it for me." He smirked.

Reluctantly, I started up the stairs.

"It will probably be fine," Sherry predicted in a half-hearted, noncommittal kind of way. Just the way people usually do in those disaster movies. The type where nobody survives.

"It's not even half your size," Leah pointed out. "Find some backbone."

I climbed the stairs, feverishly racking my brain for a reason why someone else should be doing this, but still came up empty as I reached the girls' bathroom. The door was closed and, I prayed, locked, but the handle turned easily when I tried it. I slowly, noiselessly, turned the knob, hoping not to alert or scare the Eye. I opened the door an inch and nothing happened, so I forced myself to open it the rest of the way.

A nude young woman stood in front of the mirror. Though this was astonishing, I still had had politeness beaten into me when I was young, so my reaction was automatic.

"Excuse me," I said and closed the door.

Then my mind caught up with events, and I opened the door again and stared.

The woman was studying herself in the mirror so intently that she didn't even seem to notice me. I looked around the rest of the bathroom quickly, trying to see if the Eye was hidden somewhere but turned up empty. The only sign of it was the empty box in the bathtub. I went back to staring at that vision. She was blond like Leah and about Leah's height and weight. Finally, it dawned on me, she looked exactly like Leah. She still hadn't noticed me so I closed the door and stepped back to the staircase.

Leah, Steve, and Sherry stood at the bottom of the stairs, staring up at me.

"I think you have a much bigger problem than losing your bathroom, Leah," I told her. I nodded toward the upstairs bathroom. "You have a twin."

"A twin?"

"There's no creature up here," I said. "But there is your double."

Before I could say anything more, Leah charged up the stairs. Then with the rest of us following, Leah threw open the bathroom door and skidded to a halt with an astonished look on her face.

"That looks nothing like me," she yelled.

"She's your damn double," Steve said, earning a venomous look from Leah, who was shaking her head.

Sherry just inspected the new Leah with interest.

"You do look a lot alike," I said, trying to calm Leah down. It didn't work. Her eyes narrowed and her cheeks flushed.

"I am not fat, and I don't—"

With a squeal, Leah's twin collapsed to the ground and morphed into the Eye, tentacles and all.

It was then I knew that none of us were part of reality anymore. Eyes that change into girls are not part of your standard reality. I was sure I had read that somewhere.

"See!" Leah said to us. "She looks nothing like me!"

"I can't do this," the Eye said, finally weighing in on the matter.

Seeing as how I didn't feel part of the real world at that moment, the Eye talking didn't even faze me. My housemates did not look impressed either. I was interested, however, in how it knew our language.

"You speak English?" I said in surprise.

"I'm picking it out of your mind," the Eye said. "Not that it will help any. This is all too crazy."

"This what?" I said, not sure which part of this insanity was causing our visitor a problem.

"You and your form," the Eye said. "Two legs and two arms—how strange can you get?"

"What's so strange about our form?" Leah said.

"It's all wrong!" the Eye said. "You should look just like me. Instead, you look like a bunch of monkeys or something."

"You want to tell him," Leah asked me, "or should I?"

I glanced at the distraught Eye. "I can be sensitive."

Leah looked at me dubiously. "Then you tell him, Mr. Sensitive," she said.

I tried to think of how to break it to him gently, but true to form, I blurted out the first thing I thought. "But we are monkeys....Or were monkeys at one time," I amended under Leah's amused look.

"Where are the others?" the Eye asked, "the ones who looked like me? The rulers of this planet?"

"I think that's us monkeys," Steve said.

"Where did you come from?" The Eye managed to sound outraged.

"As far as we know, we've always been here," I said. "But you were expecting someone else, weren't you?"

I was taking logic at college.

"Four tentacles and a big eye," the Eye said. "You should look just like this!"

"Sorry, Mr. Eye." Leah must have felt weird talking to a thing nicknamed the Eye. "We're all there is here."

"That's what I was afraid of." The Eye sounded crestfallen. "I think I got sent to the wrong planet!"

"How did you get here anyway?" I said. "It looked like you came with the mail."

"The box I came in was a dimensional transport shield," the Eye explained. "It protects you from the effects of dimensional projection."

"A dimensional what?" I said.

"We projected the box across dimensions to your world," the Eye said.

"So it's not a spaceship or something?" I said.

"Who can afford a spaceship?" the Eye said.

I didn't know what to say to that, so I moved to another topic.

"You said you were expecting other creatures here?" I said.

"Yes," the Eye said. "I had carefully practiced their form until I could keep it continuously. Four tentacles and a big eye. Now what am I supposed to do?"

More like, what were we supposed to do?

"Sounds like you're looking for an octopus or a squid," I offered.

"Even an octopus has two eyes, though," Leah reminded me.

"Yeah, you're definitely on the wrong planet, dude," Steve said.

The Eye teared up. "That means I'm lost," it wailed.

That was too much for me. I guess I'm a sucker for a crying eye, but I had to say something. Even if it was something like, "You may not be lost. Maybe there's an intelligent school of one-eyed squids in our oceans somewhere."

My housemates looked at me like I'd lost my mind. Which I probably had. But I felt sorry for the Eye.

"That would be nice," the Eye said. "But my creatures lived on the land like you do."

"That would make them harder to hide on this planet," I admitted. "But maybe they can change shape the way you do. I mean you appeared just like Leah—"

Leah kicked me.

"You looked a lot like Leah when I found you up here," I said.

"That was the best I could do with such a brief glimpse of her," the Eye explained. "I could do better if I saw her better."

It turned to Leah, who crossed her arms and shifted away.

"No," I said, "I was just trying to say that since you can appear like us if you want to, maybe they can as well."

"But there weren't any other intelligent species on their planet," the Eye said. "I really think that I am lost."

"I'm sorry to hear that," I said.

"So am I," the Eye said. "I'll probably never find Earth."

That moment was so weird that the doorbell ringing was anticlimactic.

As I went downstairs to answer it, Steve, Leah, and the Eye tagged along and stood around as I looked out the peephole. A tall burly man in a black suit stood outside.

"What do you want?" I asked him through the door.

"You ran a Google search on a four-legged creature with a big eye?" he said.

"We did?" I was amazed that someone had done something sensible in all this insanity.

"I did earlier," Sherry said, coming down the stairs behind us. She waved an iPad at us. "But who are you?" she asked the man through the door.

"I'd rather talk about this more privately," the man said. "Can I come in?"

"The last time we let something in the door..." Leah started.

"If you let me in, I can explain why there's a big eye in your house and I can help," the man said.

Someone to push the task off onto was too attractive to me. I let him in.

"I'm the response to your Google search," the man said. "I'm part of the government's Alien Response Force."

"ARF?" Steve said.

The man from ARF bristled.

"I'm going to pretend I didn't hear that," he said, glaring at Steve. "My name is Agent Davis."

"But I didn't find anything except other reports," Sherry said.

"Other reports?" I asked.

"Yes," she said, "all over the world people are getting surprises just like us."

I goggled at her. It hadn't occurred to me that anyone else might be going through this.

"Oh yeah," she added. "There were also reports about a book."

"A book?" I said.

"Got it right here," the Eye said, handing me a small book.

"*The Guide to Earth for Intergalactic Travelers?*" I read the front cover.

"It's been sent out on all of the recent space probes we launched," Agent Davis said, "as well as broadcasted into space."

"Earth is a planet of hyperintelligent, tentacled eyes…"

I read from the back blurb. It made an interesting tagline, I thought as I skimmed through the book. It was all there. Four tentacles and a big eye. There were even pictures and drawings of the four-tentacled creatures that looked exactly like the Eye. They were playing with Frisbees and volleyballs at the beach.

"So this book was a lure to bring aliens to Earth?" I said, amazed at the idea.

"We figured if they wouldn't come to us willingly," Agent Davis said, "we would entice them here."

"Why the four tentacles and an eye?" I wondered.

"So they would stand out," Agent Davis said. "We didn't want them to sneak in possibly looking like us and then get away. We just didn't anticipate them arriving in boxes."

He glowered at the Eye.

"We expected spaceships," he said.

"Again with the spaceships," the Eye said, sounding put-upon.

Agent Davis appeared puzzled.

"They don't exactly do spaceships," I informed him.

"How'd the package get here?" he said.

"We projected it through a dimensional warp," the Eye said. "That's the only cheap way to travel between planets."

"No spaceships, huh?" Agent Davis didn't like that. "How did you get the book without a spaceship?"

"What's so great about spaceships?" the Eye demanded.

Nobody answered. Noise coming from the backyard made the Eye hard to hear.

"Oh no," Agent Davis said rushing to the back of the house. "Not them!"

Everybody followed him, and we all watched a spaceship land in our backyard. It was actually more of a flying saucer. It settled on three legs, and a ramp came down. Then a wrinkled little gray man about four feet tall walked down the ramp and toward our back door. I would have let him in if I could.

"I can't move," I said after a few seconds of trying. Everybody else appeared stuck as well.

"That's because of the guy in the backyard. He's a gray," Agent Davis said. "They can do this thing—it's like stopping time or something. We shouldn't be awake though."

"It's the dimensional transport," the gray said as he opened the back door and walked in. "It screws up our equipment."

"You speak English too?" I said amazed.

"Translator..." the gray said, waving a small box.

"At least you have equipment and a spaceship," Agent Davis said. He was taking the Eye's lack of a spaceship hard.

"I am warden Gryxemato," the gray said to the Eye. "You and the others are hereby charged with trespassing in a protected zone."

"The others?" I said. "Are we in trouble?"

"No," the gray said. "I meant the other eyes. We've retrieved a thousand of them so far."

"That's most of us," the Eye said sadly.

"I'm glad to hear that," the gray said. "This is my tenth pickup, and I'm getting tired of it!" He glared at the Eye. "What possessed you kids to skate dimensions anyway? Especially to this planet?"

"Kids?" I said looking at the Eye.

"I'm in college," the Eye insisted. *"I'm practically grown up."*

"Only the young and foolish—" the gray started.

"And the broke…" the Eye said.

"So there *are* spaceships," Agent Davis said to the Eye. "You're just not using them."

"What is it with the spaceships?" I asked Agent Davis.

"They want one to reverse engineer," the gray said.

"Who can afford a ticket anyway?" the Eye said. "Besides, ships don't come to Earth. It's protected."

"So that's what this was?" the gray said. "A demonstration?"

"Hey, even if these humans aren't eyes," the Eye said, "I've been here for hours and nobody has attacked me. I'll bet none of the others have been hurt either."

"Earth is not protected because the people are dangerous in small groups," the gray said. "Earth is protected because the whole species is endangered."

The Eye gestured at all five of us with a tentacle. "They don't look that endangered to me."

"Currently, there are several wars on this planet," the gray said. "The number of humans dying every year puts them on the endangered species list."

"Is that why no aliens have come to visit yet?" I said.

"That's why no aliens will ever visit," the gray said. "Not until you stop killing each other and form a world government."

"Peace?" Agent Davis said. "You're waiting for peace to break out?"

"And a planetary government," the gray said. "Yes, then we will make ourselves known."

"Don't you think that this has already blown your cover?" I said, staring at the two aliens.

"Unfortunately not," the Eye said. "That's why he's here." It gestured at the gray with a tentacle.

"That's why I'm here too," Agent Davis said. "I came here hoping to contact the Eye and get him out of here before a gray arrived and wiped this whole thing from your minds." He glared at the gray. "And I almost made it."

This seemed to piss him off more than the spaceships.

I looked at the gray. "You can't just make us forget all this," I said. Could it?

"Watch me," the gray said.

Leah, Steve, and Sherry—even Agent Davis—all went glassy-eyed. They really zoned out.

"And when they return, they'll remember nothing," the gray said. "Now it's your turn."

The gray focused on me, his pupils growing larger. But I didn't feel anything. He huffed and stared some more, giving me the evil eye. I shrugged at him or I tried to, but I still couldn't move. Eyes narrowing, he stared and walked toward me, closer and closer.

Nothing. I didn't zone out or even feel tired. I didn't forget the package or the Eye. It was just too cool to forget.

"So you're naturally immune," it said after trying for some time. "There are others like that. But it won't do you any good. Nobody else will believe you."

"Is that where all those weird stories of aliens come from?" I said. "Immune people who remember?"

"Yes, but see how far you get with an insane story like this," the gray said as it grabbed the Eye and marched it to the door.

"What about the box?" I wondered.

"They degrade quickly after the occupant gets out of it," the gray said.

"It's nice to know at least one person will remember me," the Eye said as the gray dragged it away.

"Come and visit us again," I told the Eye.

"I don't think so," the gray said.

"Don't worry," my new friend called right before the door slammed. "I'll keep my eye on you."

The Authors

J. D. Cannon

After spending several decades as an engineer, teacher, and management consultant, J. D. Cannon decided to exercise the right side of his brain and try his hand at making stuff up by writing fiction.

That idea came to him in 2004 while sitting in a Florida bar and eavesdropping on some of the conversations taking place around him. He began to make up things about the people he was watching and shared these with his wife. After listening and laughing for an hour, she said "You should write a book." And so, it started.

J.D. always likes to hear from readers. Visit J.D. and check out his mystery/suspense novels at www.jdcannon.com. You can also follow him at www.twitter.com/jdcannonwrites.

Stella Donovan

Stella Donovan is a writer and editor currently based out of Silver Spring, Maryland. She is a proud graduate of University of Maryland's Jiménez-Porter Writers' House. Her fiction has been featured in Stylus: A Journal of Literature and Arts. She has twice been a prose finalist for the Jiménez-Porter Literary Prize. With the invaluable support of the of Rockville Writers' Group, she recently completed the first draft of a novel that she hopes will earn her a six-figure book deal, commercial and critical success, and a lasting place in the literary canon. If not, she'll settle for finding an agent.

Judy Kelly

Judy Kelly is an adjunct professor at Montgomery College where she has taught speech and college reading for twelve years. She enjoys bicycling, running and walking as well as the theatre, movies and museums. But her favorite pastimes are reading and writing. Her first novel, That Ever Died So Young, was published in 2014 and was a finalist in the Somerset Literary and Contemporary Fiction Award for 2014. She specializes in dialogue and has given presentations on dialogue.

S. G. Basu

S.G. Basu is an aspiring potentate of a galaxy or two. She plots and plans with wondrous machines, cybernetic robots, time travelers and telekinetic adventurers, some of whom escape into the pages of her books. Once upon a previous life on planet Earth, S.G. Basu trained to be an engineer. But since rediscovering her love of the writing and publishing her first novel in 2014, she is intent on being a prolific writer. Her zany writing habits are meticulously documented at sgbasu.com.

Spencer Stephens

Spencer Stephens does most of his writing at a wobbly pine table in his kitchen, not far from Washington, D.C. The first sign that he might become a writer came in high school; he was a ghost writer of love notes that his friends gave to the girls that they liked. He learned to love literature as an English major at East Carolina University. In 2014, Saint Pete Press published his first novel, 'Church of Golf.'

Joseph Radko Jr.

Joe Radko is an IT professional who has always loved science fiction. He spent a good part of his childhood in one book or another. Many times he would be dissatisfied with what he was reading so he would make up his own stories with their characters. From there, he began creating his own characters and stories. Then he took a creative writing course in college and has never looked back.

www.ingramcontent.com/pod-product-compliance
Lightning Source LLC
Chambersburg PA
CBHW072230190626
46809CB00017B/1685